Rowena Evans grew up in an artistic family in Sydney and has always been interested in telling stories and making pictures. As a child she thought all adults were good at drawing and that art and writing were normal occupations. She has a BA in Visual Arts and has worked as an illustrator, printmaker, writer, fairy, cartoonist and in community art, among other things.

Rowena's writing and art contain a mixture of reality and fantasy; it is always possible that something out of the ordinary may appear just around the next corner. Her hobbies include music, wandering about, reading and weeding.

Rowena Evans' work published by IFWG Publishing Australia:

As a writer and illustrator:

Sealskin Coast

DRUMS AND POWER LINES

BY
ROWENA EVANS

Drums and Power Lines
All Rights Reserved
ISBN-13: 978-1-922856-56-2
Copyright ©2016 Rowena Evans/IFWG Publishing Australia
International Reissue: 2024
V1.0

Printed in Garamond and Astrid Long.

IFWG Publishing International
www.ifwgpublishing.com
Gold Coast, Australia

Dedicated to my children Nathan, Eleanor and Miranda

To the person who gave me the idea

And to anyone else who suspects that they may have been inspiration for a character in this story

I would like to acknowledge my good friend George Jenkins, who read early drafts of the story and provided much valuable feedback and encouragement.

CHAPTER 1
DRUMS AND POWER LINES

Ivan sat on a boulder and gazed down into the valley. He felt tired to his centre; tired as the stone itself, wearing away to glittering sand. Tired of boring Willowvale. Tired of school. Tired of friends. Tired of so-called friends. The bruises and grazes of the day stung, but not as much as the memory of what Phil had said and the way everyone laughed. "You call that music? That's nothing. A baby could play that where I come from." On and on until Ivan lost his temper, embarrassed and humiliated—on to the point where at last he did what he knew Phil wanted—threw a punch—ended up grazed and sore with detention after school and the threat of a phone call to his parents next time.

Frankie lay panting beside him. "Silly old dog." Ivan rubbed her silky ears and felt as old as she did: grey about the muzzle and creaky in the bones. The view down the valley was the same as ever. Grey trees waving leaves to the breeze at the top of the ridge. Grey grass on the valley floor like worn carpet in an old house. The landscape was as dispirited as Ivan himself.

Shake yourself out of it, Ivan thought. He looked at the power lines that swooped from the ridge to the bottom of the valley. They were the only part of the view that lifted his heart. The power lines led out of the valley and toward distant hills that were far enough away to be somewhere else.

Frankie's eyes were closed. She wasn't going anywhere for a

while. Ivan put his hand into his pocket and took out his book.

It must have been the drumming that woke him. Ivan remembered reading the same page three times, and feeling the low afternoon sun warm him—feeling the rock become strangely comfortable—must have dozed—then the drumming.

"What?" Ivan sat up. Frankie was gone. "How long have I been here?" he said out loud. He stood up stiffly. Nothing was wrong at all; why did he feel so uneasy? The drumming continued insistently, rising out of the valley. "Just someone practising down there. Better go. Come on, Frankie." Ivan whistled. Trees still dawdled over the hills like flocks of straggling sheep. Grey grass still struggled to cover the earth. "Frankie! Come on! Stupid dog."

Ivan whistled again. This wasn't like Frankie. A whistle answered from the trees near the power poles, not far away. Funny sounding bird.

Frankie sat at the base of the power pole, looking up. Ivan turned toward home. She'd follow. The drumming went on and on. Ivan shook his head, trying to get the sound out of his ears. Strange. He'd never heard that sound up here before.

Feet cracked over dry sticks. Someone was running up the track. The runner came into the cleared area of the power line easement. Oh no. It was Phil. Ivan recognized his auburn hair and leather jacket, the one that had seemed so cool when Phil first hit Willowvale High School. Literally hit the school, and Ivan in particular. The buckles and strange catches of Phil's jacket glinted bright in the low-angled sunlight.

Ivan froze. Never trust Phil; never turn your back on him.

"What are you doing here? Piss off!"

Phil was older and taller than Ivan, and though he was skinny, had that quality of contained aggression that Ivan now knew from experience was backed up by solid wiry muscle. Ivan retreated towards the power pole.

"Go away," said Phil from across the clearing, breathlessness making his voice more menacing.

"I'm just leaving," Ivan started to say, when Phil wavered before his eyes like mist, and though his lips moved, his voice faded too.

Ivan rubbed his eyes and shook his head to clear his ears. Had he fainted or something? No, he was still standing. Phil was gone. Frankie whimpered and leaned on his leg.

"I thought you'd never see me."

Ivan was so surprised he took a step back, tripped and sprawled ungracefully on the ground. A girl was perched on a small platform near the top of the pole, a shaggy silhouette against the sky. Ivan didn't think he'd met her before—but he wasn't sure. All he could see was that she had a halo of golden hair, and wore a strange hairy jacket and baggy trousers. It was a small town; surely he should know her.

"Get down! You'll be electrocuted! That's a power line." Ivan forgot all about Phil, except for a misty feeling of relief that he wasn't shouting any more. He must have given up and gone away.

"I don't know what planet you just arrived from. There hasn't been electricity here for over twenty years. Come on—can't you hear it?"

"What?"

"The signal. Curfew. We have to go, now. You'd better come with me, seeing as you don't seem to know what's going on." The girl pointed to a ladder of metal spikes hammered into the wooden pole.

"You're not meant to climb the power poles, it's dangerous." Ivan stopped. He sounded like his mother. Then he noticed that the spikes went right down to the ground, didn't start three metres up the pole the way he thought they did. Hadn't he always wanted to climb up there?

"Come *on*. There's no time to waste. Listen." Ivan became aware that the drumming continued, beating faster than before. Frankie whimpered and looked over her shoulder into the bush. "Will you get up here before it's too late? Or do I have to leave you here to fend for yourself?"

"It's fine. I live just over there." Ivan pointed in the direction of home.

"For granite's sake don't be so stupid. No-one lives there. If we're not in the valley in five minutes it'll be too late. Get up here. Hurry."

"Did you see that guy, Phil, just then?"

"Stop wasting time, of course there's no-one there," snapped the girl, with a cursory glance toward the trees. "Now get up here, you idiot."

Ivan couldn't see the girl's face clearly, but her voice was so urgent that he decided to humour her. "Okay, but I'm not touching the wires." He started to climb.

"Bring the dog, stupid."

Well, at least all that skill and practise climbing trees and shed roofs and other dangerous places that Mum constantly worried about was coming in handy at last. Even with Frankie under one arm, Ivan was soon scrambling onto the platform.

"Can you do this? You'll have to carry the dog. It won't be easy. Hold this—" The girl threaded Ivan's free hand rapidly through a leather strap that hung from above. She put her own hand through another and for a moment they stood like two commuters in a city bus. "Ready? Do what I do." Not waiting for Ivan to answer, the girl leapt from the platform. For a confused instant he thought she'd fallen—but she was disappearing down the power line below a contraption whose wheels whirred down the steep curve of cable at a speed so fast that Ivan could barely hear her voice trailing after her like a ribbon. "Jump…"

"What a weirdo. I wonder why I've never seen her before." Ivan liked odd people. The girl was not only acting in an unusual and interesting way, she was dressed strangely, not identically to everyone else, the way most girls dressed. Was she really wearing a scruffy fur jacket? With cat tails hanging from it? Cool. He'd never seen anything like it. Oh well. She was gone now. Maybe he'd bump into her at school one day. She seemed to be about his age. She must be new. But for now, she was gone.

"Better go home, I guess." Ivan couldn't decide whether to put Frankie down, or disentangle his hand first.

Suddenly there was a rustle and series of cracks of breaking sticks in the bushes near the path. Frankie stiffened and growled quietly. Ivan saw movement in the bushes. Something large was crashing about there. The drumming, which Ivan had almost ceased to notice, reached a frantic pace, and then stopped. Frankie's small body shook. Ivan's hand was trapped in the leather strap. An animal emerged from the bushes, sniffed the ground, and approached the pole. It looked up, but Ivan wasn't watching it. He was off the platform and away down the cable.

The wind slapped Ivan's face. His arm ached from holding Frankie, small as she was. His other arm hurt so much that if his hand wasn't twisted into the strap he would have been struggling to hang on—would have slipped. Ivan looked down. Trees and rocks sped past below, a blur. He could hardly breathe; cold air rushed into his nose and mouth. Frankie was frozen in the crook of his elbow, a dead weight. Dead. That's what she'd be if he let go, but he was too scared to adjust his grip to a better position around the dog. In case—in case—luckily he was too busy holding on to use his imagination.

Much.

The pole that marked the bottom of the cable span appeared in Ivan's vision, rushing toward him. He could see a dark shape that was the girl—she was past the pole. His flying-fox apparatus crossed the pole's crossbar with a series of jolts, then the angle of the cable flattened. The flying fox slowed—or did it simply stop accelerating? Ivan reached the low point of the second span. The contraption definitely slowed down, though he was still moving fast. He saw the end of the line—a pole-legged structure with a platform larger than the one at the top of the ridge. Figures stood on the platform.

I must be near Leo's place. Funny that Leo never mentioned the flying fox. What a ratbag to keep that to himself. The wheels of the flying fox hit a stopper and he jerked to a halt.

"Ow!" Ivan's shoulder wrenched as his hand in the strap stopped moving before the rest of his body did. Frankie flew from his other hand with a surprised yelp, but Ivan's shoulder hurt too much for him to think about her.

Business-like hands untangled Ivan from the strap. The girl and an adult were there. A woman, though it was hard to tell from her clothes.

"Down now. Quickly."

Dazedly Ivan allowed himself to be hustled down a ladder. He remembered Frankie. "My dog—"

"She's here." The girl waited at the bottom of the ladder, holding Frankie by the collar. Ivan stared. Under that chaotic mane of hair, and even in the dimming light, she was the prettiest girl he'd ever seen.

Down in the valley, the sun was already out of sight behind the hills. It was cold. Clutching his aching shoulder, Ivan hurried after the striding figures of the woman and the girl.

Ivan tried to get his bearings. They were definitely near Leo's place. Dusk thickened, but Ivan's eyes adjusted. He could see the dirt road that ended near the power line—*How did I not get electrocuted? Maybe that was a separate cable—no power for twenty years? What did she mean?* The trees along the roadside, reassuringly, were the same as ever. It was only the people and the flying fox that were odd. *Soon we'll come to Leo's house. I'll run up and knock on the door, and ring Mum, and she'll get Dad to pick me up on his way home from work.* Ivan remembered his mobile phone and felt in his pocket for it—he could ring now—but he must have dropped it on the way down. He sighed. Ahead now, the girl carried Frankie under her arm the way Ivan carried her on the wild ride from the ridge. Ivan trotted to catch up. They were nearly at the bend below Leo's place.

"Wait!" The cold and the ride down made Ivan's legs feel shaky. "I'll carry Frankie. Wait!" He grabbed the girl's arm. "I want Frankie." He glanced up toward Leo's house. His hand fell from the girl's arm. "Where—where is it? What's happened to his house?"

Not waiting for the girl to hand Frankie over, Ivan ran up the hill toward the place where Leo's house should have stood, bumping into bushes, tripping over clumps of long grass that should not have been there. He reached the top of the slope and sat, panting, almost sobbing, on a fallen tree trunk. There was nothing there. No house. No car. No garden. No phone.

The girl was not far behind. She seized Ivan by the back of his jacket and dragged him to his feet. "Idiot," she hissed with such intensity that Ivan, halfway through twisting out of her grasp, stopped short. "Now get back to the road and follow us," she said. "Take your dog—don't let it run off if you value it—and stop risking all our lives."

What is going on? Ivan descended the slope that should have been Leo's cement driveway. *What is she talking about, risking all their lives?* He followed the girl to the road. The woman was so far ahead he couldn't see her.

"This way," grunted the girl, striding off into the dusk.

Ivan clutched Frankie to his chest and followed.

The road was one Ivan knew well. His mind raced confusedly from thought to thought. *I made a mistake about Leo's house. Just a mistake. There'll be another chance. I was stupid to come down here. That animal must have been a plain old wombat. Why run away from a wombat? I'll give these weirdos the slip and walk home. They've kidnapped me, that's what they've done...why am I doing what they say?*

The road climbed a rise, crossing an open area. Ivan looked around, hoping to see houses that would tell him exactly where he was. He'd simply missed Leo's place, just not seen it. They would come to his sister's friend Sarah's place soon. Her parents were nice. They'd let him use their phone. He'd come back tomorrow and look for his mobile. If it wasn't smashed to pieces.

"Up here." The girl left the road and entered a foot track that led up the hill between boulders. It looked remarkably like Sarah's front yard. Ivan hurried. No lights, but the house was hidden in trees...wasn't it?

CHAPTER 2
IVAN'S BRAIN HURTS

The bed was nowhere near as comfortable as the rock up on the ridge. Ivan was desperate to get to sleep. *If I am dreaming, and I go to sleep in this dream, then when I wake up I'll be back to normal,* he told himself. It didn't help him get to sleep. The more he tried, the more awake he was. He stared at the ceiling—the rafters, as there was no ceiling—until his eyes played tricks with the dim shapes of herbs and dried meat hanging above. His eyes were sore from tiredness. His shoulder ached. His stomach lumped with tough meat cooked over the fire. *Go to sleep, go to sleep. Wake up in reality.*

The fire burned to faint coals. The hut cooled. Ivan curled up tightly under a blanket that smelled of sheep. His mind jumped back to his first sight of the hut. He was so sure it was going to be Sarah's house. As they walked up the path from the road, the trees and rocks in the front yard seemed to assure Ivan that everything was normal. It was odd that there were no lights and that the wood pile was right in front of the house, that the wall of the house looked different, and wasn't Sarah's house bigger? Then Ivan was back in confusion, walking toward a primitive hut made of stones, old bricks, pieces of rusty corrugated iron and rough wood fitted into what looked like the ruins of Sarah's house. Two large dogs barked and strained at ropes. Frankie yelped. Ivan felt a stab of fear. A bearded man came out, as tall as the door opening. Like the girl and the woman, he was dressed strangely. Fire lit him from the back.

"What's got into the dogs?" the man said.

"Raven, we found a stranger," said the woman.

"It's just a boy," interrupted the girl. "He's all right. I think he's lost."

The man came out of the house and peered at Ivan in the dim light. "Who are you? Where do you come from?"

"Ivan Williams. I live just over the ridge."

"Oh, yes?" The man's voice sounded sceptical. "Thistle, you should know better. He could be from anywhere."

"Now, Raven, give me some credit for judgement. Cassie brought him down the flying fox. Do you think both of us are stupid?"

"He's strange, doesn't know anything. He didn't know about the curfew, or the flying fox, and he's scared," said the girl. "He's not dangerous."

Ivan shivered at the memory of finding Leo's house gone, and at sight of the ruins in front of him, and felt slightly insulted.

"He has to stay the night. We can't leave him out here."

"Are you sure he's not one of them?"

"He's too silly," said the girl. "And look how he's dressed. They don't dress like that. Not quite."

"It's a long time since I've seen anyone like him," said the woman. "He's not what I'd call a typical outsider."

"I just want to go home," said Ivan.

"You'd better come in," said the girl.

Inside the hut was simple, but well arranged, with a large open fireplace, and hand-made wooden furniture.

Now the girl was curled up on her bed in a corner, hidden under a kangaroo-skin rug. Her parents snored under a curtained canopy. Ivan hunched himself together for warmth. He saw Frankie on the hearthstone, and whispered her name. She stirred, jumped up and snuggled into the blanket, settled, and sighed contentedly. Ivan put his arm around her solid shape. Frankie's warmth comforted him. He felt the prickly uneven mattress against his side, just a sack filled with eucalyptus leaves; smelt its bush smell, heard its rustle. The girl's mattress rustled in reply, but she was only stirring in her sleep. Ivan saw the last glow of the coals in the fireplace.

When Ivan woke he was sure it had been a dream. He kept his eyes shut, feeling Frankie curled against him, feeling the warmth and pleasure of sleep that is experienced when half awake. It was all a vivid dream—the kind that comes at dawn. A dream of how things might be if they were not so ordinary.

An hour later Ivan was still trying to convince himself that just around the next corner everything would shift to normal. Like a person who is lost, he managed this by twists of logic. He tried convincing himself that soon everything was going to sort itself out...Okay—so he'd had some weird blackout—a sort of not-mad person's hallucination—he'd ended up with this odd family who lived like old timers in a hut. Their names weren't old-fashioned, he admitted to himself. They were probably just hippy alternate types. Cassinia and her parents, Thistle and Raven. They were kind in their abrupt, no-nonsense way. Strange that they'd no phone, and had never even heard of mobile phones.

Ivan's name caused some interest. "Williams is a name from round here," Cassie pointed out over breakfast. "Maybe he is from this area."

"I keep telling you, I live just over the ridge."

"Oh well," said Raven, "if you are really from round here we'll take you to the family when we go back to town."

Thistle and Raven worked with unhurried efficiency, eating their breakfast, packing blankets into rolls on shelves, raking the ash out of the fire, sweeping the cement floor.

"Cassie, pack up in the workshop," said Thistle.

"Come and help me," said Cassie to Ivan. She opened the door, which was locked with a primitive wooden latch. The dogs strained at their ropes outside. Cassie untied them and they greeted Frankie with sniffs.

"What are we going to do?"

"Come on." She led the way to the back of the hut, where Ivan was surprised to see another room built leaning on the main shack. Cassie opened the door. Inside, wooden objects hung from beams. Ivan felt his mouth drop open with amazement at the beautiful shapes. The air smelt of wood-shavings. He put his hand out to touch.

"What are they?"

"Don't you know?" Cassie looked at him as if he was stupid. "Thistle and Raven make musical instruments. This is their workshop." She picked one of the instruments from the bench and held it up.

Ivan felt his face redden with embarrassment. Of course he knew they were musical instruments, but ones he'd never seen before in his life. He thought of his guitar at home, his most prized possession. Some of the instruments here were kind of similar. "A banjo? A violin? I'm not sure. Is that a flute?" He pointed, and felt foolish. He loved music. He should know the names of these.

"We don't call them anything much. Just musical instruments. The people who buy them give them names."

"Can I try one?"

"Not now. It's not the time." Cassie took a leather bag from under the bench and gently placed the instrument in it. "Hold this." She took another, differently shaped, from a hook on the wall and packed it into another bag that was made from leather with balding remnants of fur on the inside. "We'll take them back to town. Selling them tonight."

"Oh." Ivan didn't understand, but he wanted to look intelligent. He ran his hand over the curves of one of the unfinished forms.

"They're beautiful. Can you play them?" His fingers itched to have a go. The strings plunked quietly as Cassie handled the leather bags, as if the instruments couldn't wait to be played.

"Yeah, of course."

"Show me."

"Okay." Cassie sighed and picked up an instrument. She played a surprisingly elaborate tune.

"Wow. That's fantastic. Play something else."

"Some other time. Not now, I told you. We have to go."

While they carefully packed up several more instruments all the questions that had been building up inside Ivan since he first saw Cassie poured out of him: Why don't I already know you? Are you new in town? Do you go to school? Are you home-schooled? Do your parents work in town? He was sure anyone as unusual-looking as Cassie should have come to his attention; she should be his friend already. "Do you live here in the hut all the time?"

Cassie answered only the last of Ivan's questions. "No. Of course not. We come out here for a break, and when we make the instruments. You know what it's like in town."

Ivan had no idea what she meant. He knew what it was like in town, but clearly his impressions were different from hers. Now he guessed he'd asked all the questions Cassie was going to tolerate. More answers would be hard to come by. He silently picked up the instruments that she handed him, and slung them around his shoulders.

During the short journey to town Ivan forced himself to admit that something was definitely different. He could convince himself that he was disoriented, that he'd had a strange, dreamlike episode where the imaginary flying fox and the animal seemed real, that he was mistaken about the exact location of Leo's and Sarah's houses...that he'd stumbled on a hippy-ish hermit family who lived somewhere remote but close, who were strange but familiar...and yet...

As he trailed behind Cassie, Thistle and Raven, Ivan could no longer convince himself that this strange world was the normal, everyday place he lived in. That didn't make anything less confusing. If this was somewhere else, why did this landscape look exactly like home? He just couldn't imagine that the road he walked on wasn't the one that led past Leo and Sarah's houses; the same street that led to the dog pound and the sewage works, the one that led to the bottom of the big span of power lines sweeping down from the ridge.

Piles of bricks and scrap dotted the sides of the road. They looked as if they had once been houses that he knew. He looked away. What had happened? Had there been a war in the night? No, of course not. He would have noticed. Ivan shook his head to make his thoughts behave, and caught a glimpse of yet another ruined house. After that he kept his eyes on the ground.

"Nearly there, cheer up." Cassie waited for him. She pointed. Where the oval should have been, if this was Willowvale, was a fenced field sparsely planted with scraggly vegetables. Further away he saw a fortified town like something out of a book.

Ivan gave up trying to work things out. He could neither make anything fit, nor make it not fit. Everything was different, yet the same—the same, yet different. He felt shaky. "Please tell me. I thought I knew, but I don't. Where are we?"

"Willowvale, of course."

A bright idea occurred to Ivan. Maybe somehow he'd travelled in time but not space. *Was this what the olden days were really like? Perhaps…*"Well, then, what date is it? Tell me."

"The eighteenth of August."

"Yes, but what year?"

"Two thousand and—" Cassie named the current year—"of course. Don't you know anything?"

Ivan sighed. "It can't be."

"Can you two hurry up? We haven't got all day."

They crossed the creek by a ford and continued toward the town. All the flat floodplain land was ploughed and fenced. No sports oval. No football goals or cricket pitch. No netball rings.

Ivan was so confused that when he saw the old gaol exactly as it always was at home, its high granite walls looming over the road, he once more switched to thinking that everything was normal. He imagined rounding the corner and seeing the street as he knew it: cars parked nose to kerb, people climbing the steep Post Office steps, parcels and letters in their hands. He imagined seeing the green iron fence of the war memorial, the pub on the corner, the supermarket.

No. The wall continued from the gaol corner, not neatly made from straight stone like the gaol wall, but of a mixture of uncut stones, wood and scrap metal, topped with teeth of broken glass. The wall was interrupted by a large archway, gate raised like a castle portcullis. Inside Ivan saw a narrow street with buildings crowded close. He gasped.

The street would have been interesting—Ivan would have loved it—if only it was somewhere else. Like in a film. It looked like a film set. People stared. Ivan stared back. Cassie's jacket looked more outlandish here than in the bush: its many tails swung from her waist as she walked. Raven and Thistle's jackets were just as wild. Raven, Thistle and Cassie had crazy manes of light coloured hair, while the people in the town all had neat, combed hair; women and girls wore their hair tied back or plaited. The family wore baggy woollen trousers, while the townspeople mostly wore more conventional clothes that reminded Ivan of something—old photos? Gran when she was younger? Pop in his going-to-town outfit?

Ivan tried to look inconspicuous. He was wearing ordinary jeans, a long sleeved T-shirt with a picture of his favourite band printed on it and his colourful hooded jacket. *Nothing out of the way. Until today.* Okay, his hair was a bit different from the hair of the boys who stared at him, whose hair looked like…well, they all had short back and sides like old men. He already knew that Thistle thought his clothes odd, and if she thought it, well he guessed other people would think them odder.

Ivan followed Thistle, Raven and Cassie through the maze of streets, strange smells and sights bouncing off his overloaded senses. There were horses, but no stagecoaches; there were some women in long skirts and nearly all the men had beards, but they didn't look like men or women from the olden days. More like an incompetent, home made theme-park version of the olden days where nobody knew what period they were copying.

They left the busy streets near the gate and soon arrived at an old house that looked quite normal. Ivan breathed a sigh of relief. The last time he saw the house, it was not crowded between sheds and vegetable patches and fruit trees, and didn't have a large goat tethered at the front step. It was certainly the same house, though, he was sure.

"This is my grandparent's house!"

Thistle and Raven exchanged a relieved glance.

CHAPTER 3
GRAN, POP, AND
ESPECIALLY MICK

As he climbed the front stairs, Ivan saw the familiar things that he saw each time he visited Gran and Pop—pot plants on the veranda, a pair of Pop's boots by the door, old cane chairs placed so that someone sitting there could watch the street in comfort, a place for a cup of tea on the wobbly table.

Ivan knocked, his heart thumping. Now Gran would come, he'd have a glass of lemonade and a biscuit like always, and he'd ring Mum and Dad to pick him up. He forgot Cassie, Thistle and Raven, who stood silently behind him, and the strangeness of the town. Ivan's heart beat so loudly he thought it was Pop's heavy footsteps in the hall.

No answer. He knocked again.

"Wait a minute. I'm coming."

Yes! It was Pop's voice, sounding cranky. Ivan bounced on his toes. "Pop! It's me!"

"Just wait a mo," grumbled Pop's voice. "Marg, where's the key?" There was a pause. The family behind Ivan continued to stand silently. He wondered why they stayed. Everything was sorted now. He kept his eyes on the textured glass panel in the front door. Through it the hallway of the house was a shadowy cave, Pop moving near the door, and emerging from the kitchen at the end of the hall another figure that looked like Gran. She reached the door, and the lock rattled. The door opened, creaking.

Yes! There were Gran and Pop. Ivan lurched forward and hugged Gran tightly. "I'm so glad to see you," he said, loosening his hug from her stiff shoulders.

Gran said nothing.

Ivan turned to hug Pop too.

"No, young fellow." Pop backed away. Gran was inching away too, closing the door as she did.

"Stop—he says—he knows you," said Cassie suddenly.

"Never saw him before in my life," said Pop.

"No, never." Gran folded her arms across her chest.

"Of course you have! I was here last weekend." Ivan tried to take Gran's hand, which she withdrew as if afraid he'd burn her. Pop pushed at the door, but Ivan shoved his foot into the gap.

Ivan twisted round to Cassie and her parents, keeping the door open with difficulty. "What's wrong with them? Are they crazy or something? Ow, stop it, Pop, you're hurting me."

"Come on, Charlie. Open up. He's a relation of yours all right," called Raven.

"Nope."

"Just have a look at him. He looks like one of the family if you'll only have a look at him."

"I've seen more than enough of him," said Gran through the gap between the door and its frame. "Hugging people he's never met."

"Don't you know me? Ivan—Charles—Alexander—Williams," yelled Ivan. Had they been struck by sudden madness? "My father is your son. Michael—Charles—Williams. Your son."

Suddenly the door snapped open.

"You liar." The old people looked past Ivan to Raven, Thistle and Cassie. "What the hell do you think you're up to? Get off my property with this…this…"

"Michael Charles Williams is my father! You're my grand-parents!" yelled Ivan again.

"I'll settle you. Stirring up gossip and strife," said Gran. "What will people think?" Indeed, a small group of people were watching with interest from the footpath, almost leaning on the garden gate in their efforts to hear what was going on. Grandma turned toward the back of the house. "Mick! Mick! Get here, will you?"

A voice called from the back of the house. "Coming." The back door slammed.

"He's my father. He'll know me—" said Ivan loudly.

"Keep your voice down," said Gran.

"No, I won't."

"Calm down, Ivan." Thistle put her hand on Ivan's arm. "We need to sort this out calmly."

"He's my father. You're all mad," Ivan muttered. "They're not calm. They're demented." Out loud he said, "He'll tell you. My dad will tell you even if you've forgotten me."

Pop broke into the conversation. "Who's your mother then, boy? Tell me that."

"You know her—don't pretend you don't—" The shape of a man came closer in the shadows of the hall, a silhouette. "Dad! It's me! Tell them. They're all crazy. Haven't you been worried?"

Pop repeated his question. "Who's your mother, boy?"

Ivan watched the well-known shape of his father approach, his footsteps sounding the same as ever. It was him all right. Absently he replied, "Elena—Anne—Alexander." As he said it, he realized that it caused no particular reaction. Nobody responded to this statement. All were watching as Mick opened the door wide and placed himself in front of Pop and Grandma.

"What's going on?"

"Mad people at the door. Get rid of them, will you, dear?"

"Dad!"

Mick came onto the veranda. Ivan stepped back, though he was never afraid of his father. He looked the same, but like so many things here, worryingly different. His clothes were old and patched. He seemed thinner. His hair was greyer, and his face more worn than it should have been. But it was definitely him.

"Now, what's happening? Ah, Raven, Thistle. Good morning. Hello, Cassie."

"Dad! I'm here!"

"This boy's got a screw loose," called Gran from behind.

"Stop teasing me, Dad. You tell them. Tell them. Did you call the police? Is Mum here? I'm sorry if you were worried. Can we go home now? I didn't mean—"

Dad, or Mick, seemed confused. "I've never met any Elena Alexander that I can remember. I don't have any kids your age. What's your name again?"

"Ivan Williams. My name's Ivan Charles Alexander Williams. The same surname as you. You should know. I'm fifteen years old, remember? I live at twenty-five Bruno Street, Willowvale. My mother is Elena and my father is you." Ivan repeated this information remembering the way his mother had taught him when he was very young. He stopped himself from reciting his phone number and tried not to think of Mum. How worried she must be. In fact, why wasn't she here at Pop and Gran's? Maybe she was out the back, waiting by the phone, and didn't hear the knock on the door. Or perhaps she was at the police station…or maybe she and Dad had had a fight and that was why he was acting so oddly…

"Stop it at once, boy," said the grandmother.

"You must be mistaken," said Dad, or Mick, in a kind, slow voice. "My daughters are older than you. My wife's name is Penny. We've got grandchildren. You're not my child. There's no Bruno Street in this town. Not any more."

"No." Ivan looked round at Cassie and her parents. Now they

seemed more like people he knew than these strange, unwelcoming grandparents and the worn-out, reasonable father telling lies. He felt as if the ground was falling away beneath his feet. Thistle put her hand on Ivan's arm again. "Come home with us, we'll sort it out somehow."

"Sorry, Ivan," said Mick.

"Troublemakers," said Pop.

"Don't you go around telling such lies," said Gran.

"I'm not lying," said Ivan.

"Troublemakers," said Pop again.

"They're not troublemakers. They're my friends, they're good people," said Ivan.

"My friends too. Forget it, Dad." Mick smiled at Raven and Thistle.

Cassie, who already had Ivan by the elbow, shepherded him down the veranda steps, the leather instrument bags banging hollowly on his back. The old people slammed the door shut. Mick came down the steps.

The dogs stretched. Frankie, luckily, had made friends with the big dogs. Ivan gave the goat a wide margin, untied Frankie from the apple tree that wasn't in the front garden he knew, and followed the others to the gate. The knot of people still stood there, staring.

"Who's the boy?" someone asked.

"Cousin from the mountains," said Raven.

They pushed through the small crowd. Close up, Ivan decided that people were odder than he had first thought. Some wore clothes of an out-dated fashion, but patched over and over with other materials. Some men wore simple woollen trousers like those Raven, Thistle and Cassie wore, with shirts of all sorts of fabrics under hand-spun jumpers. The women were mostly dressed in hand-woven woollen skirts, though some wore jeans so patched the original fabric was barely visible. The people's shoes were similarly a mixture of old and patched, and home-made. Some wore sheepskin boots or moccasins, and some people had shoes soled with pieces of car tyre. They wore old overcoats, shabby ski parkas and scarves. All the people stared shamelessly at Ivan as he came out onto the footpath.

"Come on, follow us," said Cassie.

Ivan turned to look back at Gran and Pop's house. Dad—Mick—waved from the gate. Ivan found it difficult to stop looking at him—and it seemed that Mick felt the same, for each time Ivan turned back he was standing at the gate, watching. The staring people thinned and dispersed, but Mick stood there until Ivan went around a corner and lost sight of him.

Thistle and Raven led the way rapidly through the town. Ivan saw many buildings he recognized: houses and shops looking run-down and shabby—but what he knew as open space in the town was filled in with small sheds and shanties, vegetable gardens, wood piles, fruit trees, stables and chook runs. Everything smelled of animals and wood smoke.

As he walked, Ivan's mind whirled. A procession of conflicting images passed his eyes, and at the same time in his mind's eye his father watched him walk away from Pop and Grandma's house—puzzled, unwilling to look away. They reached the park in the centre of town—tall trees and the bandstand looked the same as usual, but the main street had not a car in it except the back tray of a ute made into a cart, pulled by two oxen. The street was occupied by horses, not cars. Shops looked the same—sort of—but some had their plate glass windows curtained or boarded; some had dismal, unsaleable-looking items in boxes on display. There was rusty scrap metal, ancient clothes, turnips, hand-spun jumpers, leather hats, sheep and goatskins. Horses were everywhere, tied to faded but ordinary street signs that said *Loading Zone* or *1 Hour Parking 8:30a.m.—6:00 p.m. Monday to Friday*. There were horses carrying people and pulling carts of all shapes. Ivan saw a cart pulled by a goat, and a girl leading a donkey loaded with sticks tied together with rope. Yet some things did look quite normal. The pub on the corner still had *Drover's Arms 1896* over the door, and when Ivan peered into the dim bar he surely saw some figures that as far as he remembered were always there. The only decent-looking shop was opposite the park. *Bagshaw Enterprises* said the large red and white sign above the door. As they passed, Ivan saw new things in the window—tins of paint, kettles, and a vase of artificial flowers. *Service is our business* was painted on the shiny window.

The family strode ahead with their big dogs. They nodded greetings to a few people in the street, though Ivan noticed most people staring almost as curiously at them as they did at him. Ivan was already behind. Frankie struggled to keep up with her silly short legs. Ivan couldn't stop the image of Dad—Mick—appearing in his mind, on the veranda, not knowing him, saying he had a different family, grandchildren. Yet Mick kept looking at Ivan as if he reminded him of something forgotten, something packed away in the back cupboard of his memory, covered in dust and cobwebs.

I have to talk to him again. What am I doing following like a dog? Strangely, Ivan suddenly thought of a game he still played sometimes with Anna, his little sister. The game where you stand on the grass and spin around and around until the world looks like nothing but blurry stripes of colour—around and around—until at last you fall over and the ground turns over you like a tsunami that won't break and you don't know which way is up and the world still spins and you feel a bit sick. Ivan felt slightly sick now. It might have been the smell of horse manure that was everywhere, but he knew it was the spinning of thoughts, sights, expectations, smells, and the feeling of the earth turning itself over him, but not crashing down.

The others were a block ahead now. The streets in the centre of town were laid out the same old way. Ivan knew them. *I've got to talk to Dad—Mick*, he thought. He was opposite a laneway that led from the main street though to a car park and the street behind. It was only a short walk back to Gran and Pop's. Ivan picked Frankie up and ducked into the lane. He started to run, skidding around puddles still frozen in the shadows, past a dark shed that looked and sounded like the blacksmith's shop from the gold-rush place where they replicated the olden days, out of the lane at a fenced yard full of horses and donkeys, not a car park as it should have been. Ivan turned into the street at the end of the lane, dropped Frankie, and headed back toward Pop and Gran's house, Frankie panting behind.

People in the back street stared at him, but no more than before, and Ivan was getting used to it. By the time he reached the corner near the house, hurrying all the way, Ivan was sweating despite the cold air that dried his throat.

"I hope he's in the back yard," Ivan muttered to Frankie. He picked her up again. Lucky Pop and Gran lived in the old part of town full of back lanes and short cuts. The lane behind their place was piled with rusty scrap metal not unlike what Ivan knew was always there. He found what he thought was the back of Gran and Pop's place. A curly old garden gate that had been repaired with ragged chicken wire interrupted the paling fence. It looked like one that Ivan vaguely remembered from when he was very young. The sound of an axe on wood punctuated more distant sounds—horses' hooves on the road, the distant ring of the blacksmith's hammer. Ivan peered over the gate but a shed obscured his view into the yard. Was this the right house? No time to waste, but it would be bad to burst in on a complete stranger…how long until Raven, Thistle and Cassie came looking for him? Was it Pop or even Grandma cutting firewood, not Dad—Mick? Ivan wanted to talk to him—had to talk to him. What should he do? As these thoughts straggled across Ivan's mind like chooks in a back yard, Dad's voice joined the layers of sound that reached Ivan's ears. He was singing in rhythm with his axe strokes. A song Ivan knew.

Ivan opened the gate. It creaked like a gang-gang's cry. The singing stopped. "Who's there?"

Ivan clutched Frankie to his chest and stepped down the path, past the out-house. Dad—Mick—stood at the woodpile.

"You."

"I need to talk to you."

"Where are you from? Ivan, isn't it?"

"You really don't know me?"

"I'd send you off in a second," said Mick thoughtfully, "but something about you bothers me. I don't mean the 'father' thing. Let's forget that for now. But you remind me of someone—someone in the family? You do look as if you belong some way or other." He leaned the axe carefully against an ancient grindstone that Ivan knew usually lived with other junk in the back of Pop's shed. "Don't push me. Where are you from, boy?" Mick shoved the hair off his forehead, stretched and moved as if to pick up the axe and chop more wood.

Ivan looked at his father's face, silent. He felt as if he was standing on the edge of a cliff with nothing at its base.

"Well? Are you going to tell me?"

"I'm from Willowvale. But the Willowvale I'm from is different. In that one, you're my father. Pop and Gran are my grandparents." Ivan didn't realize he was squeezing Frankie more and more tightly until she whimpered. He looked down and saw his fingers, white from clutching Frankie's body; he put her down and she leaned against his leg. "Everything there is the same but different. The hills are the same. The park is the same. The streets are the same. Even some of the people are the same. You, Gran, Pop...men in the pub...but there's no wall, there are no curfews...no ruins, no horses..." Ivan's voice faltered as he put thoughts to words. His throat hurt. He put his hand over his mouth for a moment, looked down at Frankie, whose eyes searched his face for reassurance. "I don't know what's happened. I can't understand anything, and you're the one who can help me. I want to go home…" Ivan wiped the back of his hand across his face roughly and looked at Dad—at Mick—

Mick's face was as pale as Ivan's. He put the axe down again. "You'd better come inside," he said.

CHAPTER 4
ONE OF THE FAMILY?

Ivan followed Mick up the back step, across the closed-in veranda. They paused at the door to wipe their boots.

"Tea's in the pot, Mick," said Gran from inside.

"Put out another cup, could you, Mum, we've got a visitor."

"Not another one," said Gran. "I've had enough visitors for one day."

Mike and Ivan came into the kitchen. At first glance it looked the same as ever. Gran and Pop never were ones for pointless renovations. The wood stove that Gran refused to replace was lit and the old kettle steamed gently on the back of the stovetop. Ivan realized it was the first really warm place he'd been in since the sun went down yesterday. He was shivering; he didn't know whether it was from the cold. However this was no time to think of warmth or to look around the kitchen properly.

Gran and Pop sat at the table.

"What's he doing here again?" said Pop.

"I swear I've never seen him before, but you have to have a good look at him." Mick pushed Ivan toward the table.

"Just some feral kid trying to get a free feed," said Gran, putting down her mug.

"No." Dad—Mick—spoke the way he spoke to Ivan in that other life, when Ivan said something stupid. "Look at him." He grabbed Ivan by the elbow and pulled him toward the window where the light was good. Pop and Gran were silent. "You can see it, can't you? But I'd swear by the oldest tree in Willowvale that he's nothing to do with me."

Gran put both hands on the table and stood up slowly, her eyes on Ivan, her mouth shut in a straight line. She said nothing, searching Ivan's face. Pop drained his tea in a gulp and put the mug down with a bump, looking at the tabletop. Gran turned abruptly and left the room.

"Look at him, Dad," said Mick, angrily. He shook Ivan's elbow.

Pop looked, his face expressionless. He too remained silent. Ivan forced himself to look into Pop's eyes. The old man gave nothing away—but Ivan thought he saw his eyes flick from him to Mick, then back in a surprised movement.

Gran reappeared, carrying a large book. She put it on the table. "Sit down." She went to the cupboard and took out a mug, put it on the table next to one ready for Mick, topped up the tea pot from the kettle, replaced the kettle on the stove, sat down, and poured two cups of tea.

Ivan sat down between Gran and Mick. Pop poured himself more tea, not taking his eyes from Ivan and Mick.

"Have a look at this." Gran pushed the book across the table to Mick. Ivan's hand began to shake and he put his mug down so he wouldn't splash tea onto the cloth. He knew the album. He, his young sister and Anna and their older sister Reenie loved looking at it, because it was the album with photos of Dad when he was young. Ivan had seen it many times.

Slowly Mick opened the album. There were old black and white photos on the first pages. All of them were exactly the same as those in Gran's album at home. Gran and Pop's wedding, this house when they bought it, their first car. A baby: Dad. Mick turned the pages deliberately, not hurrying. Everyone's eyes were on the photos. Dad as a toddler. Pop holding Uncle Jack as a tiny baby. Dad's first day of school at Willowvale Public, in long socks with stripes around the top that matched an inexpertly knotted tie. "I wanted to do it myself," Dad always said when he saw it. Aunty Sue as a tiny baby, Dad and Uncle Jack looking at her in a young Grandma's arms, the boys wearing uncertain expressions. The family on holidays at the beach, squinting into the sun. In coloured photos with the blue fading out of them: at the river, in the back yard, growing up. Dad's first day of high school in another too-big school uniform—no tie this time. Ivan held his breath. Dad—Mick—picked up the corner of the page. Ivan knew what was coming. Whenever anyone saw the photo, they looked again. "Crikey," or "Wow!" or whatever their habit, they would say, "Is that you, Mick? Ivan is the living image of you at that age."

Mick turned the page. There it was. Dad gazed out of the photograph, fifteen years old, with a face so like Ivan's it took the breath away. Mick, Grandma and Pop pulled the album toward them, stared at the photo, then with one movement turned to look at Ivan.

"It's incredible," said Pop.

"Nobody can dispute it," said Gran slowly. Her eyes slid sideways toward Mick. Ivan almost saw questions form in her mind, though she didn't ask them. *Are you sure you don't have any other children? Should Penny know about this? Is there something you haven't told me, son?*

Mick shook his head as if Gran had spoken.

"Can I see more?" asked Ivan. Mick slid the album to him. The others watched in silence as he turned the next few pages. All the same photos as ever. Aunty Sue holding a puppy. Uncle Jack with a large fish dangling from a fishing line, huge grin nearly splitting his face. Ivan laughed. "Just after that the fish flapped and he fell in the river," he said, repeating the old story that always went with that photo. Gran, Pop and Mick all gasped and Mick coughed as he swallowed hot tea the wrong way. Next was Dad holding up his school certificate, Dad in clothes that were probably cool at the time, with a girl at a school dance.

Ivan turned the page, absorbed in something completely familiar. He felt three sets of eyes on him. They wanted to know his thoughts, but even he didn't know them. Ivan carefully grasped the corner of the page and turned it.

Nothing.

No photos of Uncle Jack and Aunty Sue leaving school. He turned another page. No photos of Dad's friends from university. No photos of Mum, no Grandma and Pop on their caravan trips around Australia. Blank.

Ivan looked quickly at the next page, his heart racing. Now there were different pictures. Little pencil sketches of babies, not very well drawn, with unknown people's names written below: Cathy, Michelle. There was an ink drawing of Gran and Pop's house with the fruit trees in the front garden, small saplings. On the next page were silhouettes made from cut-out paper, one of Pop, the other of Gran.

Ivan looked at the three people watching him. "What on earth happened? Where are the rest of the photos?"

"What others? There are no other photographs—not since the disaster."

"Disaster? Do you mean the flood when I was a baby? That wasn't that bad, was it?"

"That flood wasn't as much as a pimple on an elephant's back. How could you not know about the meteorite destroying Walagu, wrecking Stirling...how we've been cut off since then when the outsiders from O'Malley turned on us. Where have you been? Living under a rock?" Pop's voice was full of contempt.

"More tea? You look as though you need it," said Grandma, who looked rather in need of tea herself.

Ivan was confused. *What meteorite? What disaster? Cut off?* O'Malley turning on Willowvale? It meant nothing to him. He went back through pages of the album. There was Dad's young face, smiling out of the photos like a reflection. Experimentally, Ivan turned the page to see if it had changed back to normal. Nothing. Blank; a gap. Then unfamiliar pictures.

"Life changed a lot after the meteorite, boy."

Ivan became aware that someone was knocking on the door, and had been for—for how long? Pop, Gran and Mick looked as if they had not heard it until that moment, either. Mick went to the door.

"Is Ivan here? He got lost." It was Cassie, anxious. Mick showed her in. Gran poured her a cup of tea.

Pop ignored Cassie, intent on saying to Ivan, "You know the album. You look the way you look—but things are the same here as they've always been—there are no photographs—now."

Cassie saw the photo of the young Mick as Pop leafed through the pages. Like the others, she gasped. "Wow. He looks exactly like you! So he is your relation! He must be some sort of distant cousin or nephew or something!"

"He knows everything about us before the disaster. Nothing about us since it," said Gran, clapping her mouth shut as if regretting the unguarded moment, then repeated, "Yes, distant cousin…"

"Everyone knows Mick. The boy can't possibly be his. Yet—" said Pop, then snapped his mouth shut too.

They stared at Ivan.

"I don't know anything…I do know things. I know what I know…that's all. I'm as confused as you are."

Gran studied Ivan speculatively. "The meteorite. It must have something to do with it. Like Pop said, things changed then."

"This is very interesting," said Cassie, "but Thistle is worried. Do you want to keep him? Or shall I take him?"

"I'm not a dog, you know."

"Your parents don't mind?" Mick asked Cassie.

"They like him. Don't know why," said Cassie. Ivan turned his eyes to her as quickly as he could and saw the tail end of a smile cross her face.

"Probably better," said Pop. "He can't possibly be yours, Mick, but it might upset Penny and the girls to see him with that face before they are warned."

Ivan felt slightly insulted. Pop was still turning the pages of the album, and as he said this the page with Dad at the Year 10 social opened. "Penny! The girl in the photo! Mrs Thompson! I know her."

"That settles it," said Pop, standing up. "You'd better go with Cassie, boy."

"Yes, it would be better," said Gran. "Go with Cassie, dear."

"We must go," said Cassie. She drank the tea quickly and stood up. "Thank you for the tea, Mrs Williams."

Ivan and Mick stood also. Frankie jumped up from a warm spot by the stove, and stretched. At the door, Mick said to Ivan, "Come again. Mum and Dad won't mind. The back lane, back door's the best."

Cassie said quietly to Mick, "There's a dance at the old school hall tonight. Coming?"

"Don't know. I'll see. You know what it's like."

Cassie strode off down the street. Ivan hurried to catch up.

"You walk a lot, don't you?" Ivan asked Cassie.

"How else can you get around?"

"Cars, of course."

"Cars?" Cassie laughed. "Have you seen any cars here?"

"Bikes, then, do you have bicycles?"

"Oh yes, some people have them. But not many. It's too hard to replace the parts if they go wrong."

Ivan looked around. They were in a quiet street. Now that he thought about it, the only cars he'd seen were rusting wrecks with all the removable parts missing, or carcases cut up and made into something else, like the trailer pulled by a horse down the main street. He looked around, and saw piles of horse manure in the gutter. "Horses, then?"

"More trouble than they're worth unless you have a lot to carry," said Cassie. "We know one or two people who own them, but not everyone has one."

Ivan whistled to Frankie to hurry her up. Cassie certainly could walk fast. Frankie's little legs were a blur. "Wait! Is it far?"

Cassie paused to wait. As Ivan and Frankie caught up, she laughed. "There's a car for you." Ivan looked where she pointed. Over a fence he saw a derelict car, its glassless windows filled with tangled wire. Hens clucked inside. "You won't get far in that. Easier to walk."

"Don't cars exist at all here? I mean, ones that work?"

Cassie started walking again. Ivan had to almost trot to keep up. "Well, not really. Sometimes they come in from O'Malley." She named a city about a hundred kilometres away. "There's a bit of trade from there…usually trucks, not cars. Trucks, you know, like big carts, but without horses. Smelly things. We trade with the outsiders sometimes, but it's frowned upon." Cassie said the word outside as if it had a capital letter, the way Gran and Pop had talked about the meteorite.

Ivan was curious, but Cassie spoke in a tone of voice that implied she didn't want to discuss trucks or O'Malley. He changed the subject. "What's this dance you were talking about?"

"Shh! Keep your voice down, you idiot."

"What?"

Cassie grabbed Ivan's wrist and looked around. Across the street a teenage girl and a woman walked together. They stared at Ivan. Cassie walked even faster.

"Stop dragging me." Ivan twisted his arm and freed it from Cassie's grip. He was taller than her, but she was strong. "Are you demented?"

"You be quiet. Just walk, then. That girl over there listens everywhere and tells everything. Jess. Huh."

"It's just a dance at the school hall, what's the stress?"

"Shut up."

"Come on, we were looking at a photo of a school dance a few minutes ago. What's the problem?"

Cassie gave Ivan a withering glance and strode ahead. Luckily Ivan kept his eye on her, for suddenly she turned a corner, and then almost immediately turned again, in through a solid, high wooden gate partly hidden in the greenery of a tall cypress hedge. Picking up Frankie, Ivan went in after her. Cassie slammed the gate shut and bolted it. "Just be quiet when I tell you. This town isn't the fairy tale you seem to think it is. Now come inside, Thistle has been frantic."

Like Gran and Pop's front yard, Thistle, Raven and Cassie's was full of many things. There were fruit trees and a large vegetable garden instead of a front lawn. Paths branched to a corrugated water tank covered with vines, a small shed with a chimney, and to a pen full of ducks, which quacked in fright at the slamming of the gate. Mostly the yard was full of the same kind of things as Gran and Pop's, and gardens Ivan had seen on his way through the town. Practical things. However, unlike Gran and Pop's the vegetable beds here were laid out in a decorative pattern. There were other things as well. Sculptures made of scrap metal and oddly shaped wood. A pond with water lilies. A small, rather dry lawn with a bench under a bush that Ivan knew in spring would be covered in flowers. There was even a tall gum tree with a tyre swing hanging from its lowest branch. Ivan had a childish urge to try it. The whole place was enclosed by the hedge.

"Wow. What a great garden."

"Come on." Cassie hurried up the main path, and followed the front of the house, which was made of chalky red bricks, and ducked into a narrow side path that led past a bed of berry canes and a grape vine to the rear of the house. It was one of the old houses in Railway Street. The back garden was similar to the front, full like the other yards of useful and productive plants. It also contained a sundial and a small pond overhung with iris plants. There was a large wood pile, a compost heap and a shed, as well as a small structure that was no doubt an outdoor toilet, and a washing line already hung with a few dripping items of hand-spun clothing. Ivan knew that on the other side of the high corrugated iron back fence was the disused railway line. The two dogs lay in the sun on the back pathway like large shaggy rugs.

"Come in, then." Cassie was still angry with Ivan, and he still had no idea why.

"I found him. At the Williams' place."

"Oh, good." Thistle's voice came from a distant room.

"Wait here," said Cassie to Ivan.

Ivan waited. He heard Cassie speaking to Thistle and Raven, but he could not tell what they were saying. Soon Cassie returned to the kitchen.

"Get some wood and light the fire, will you, Cassie," called Thistle after Cassie as she entered. "I haven't had time yet, what with this and that, and we need something hot for lunch." Then Ivan heard her voice and Raven's.

"Do your parents always order you around like this?" whispered Ivan.

Cassie looked at him without replying to this remark. "Come on. You can help." They went to the woodpile and filled two cracked plastic buckets with twigs. "You carry these," said Cassie. She loaded his arms with cut logs and they stomped back to the house.

"Put some kindling in the stove." She pointed at an old wood-fired stove, very like Gran's, but not as shiny.

"Where's some newspaper to start it off?"

"Don't be silly. You don't burn paper. Chuck some leaves in."

Ivan saw a box of dry gum leaves by the stove. He laid the fire carefully—he didn't want to look incompetent. Lucky he was used to lighting the fire at home—*don't think about home*, he reminded himself as he worked.

Cassie peeled potatoes at the table and put them into an old saucepan that she filled from the rainwater tank.

"Where are the matches?"

"On the shelf, see, the top one."

Ivan found them, a brand he'd not seen before, their box strangely bright against the silvery neutral colours of the kitchen: old lino, faded paint, greying wood. He struck a match. It snapped at the head and didn't light. Ivan struck another.

"Hey! Don't waste matches, stupid."

"They're just matches."

Cassie dropped her potato and snatched the second match, which was now burning, from Ivan. Quickly she held it to the dry leaves in the stove and breathed out with relief as they caught and flamed. "At least you can lay a fire," she said quietly.

"I'm not stupid. Why do you think I am? Why are you mad with me? I don't understand."

Cassie turned on him so fast her wild straw-coloured hair swung round and whipped Ivan's face. She swiped it roughly away from her eyes. "You don't know anything. You yell out things that are secret in the street. You didn't know what the drums mean. You don't know about danger. You didn't know about the flying fox. You thought some Leo person would be where there's never been a house. You think old Mr and Mrs Williams are your grandparents and they've never set eyes on you. Let alone poor Mick Williams. What on earth can you be thinking? What will his wife say? How will his children feel? And you think it's all right to waste matches. You're not just stupid, you're a complete idiot. I wish I hadn't saved you." Her voice sank to a fierce whisper.

"I wish you hadn't too. I'd be at home now." Ivan threw the box of matches to the floor and they spilled across the hearth.

"Don't—they come from O'Malley. Bagshaw's only get them in once a month, and they cost a fortune." Cassie knelt down and picked the matches up carefully, including the broken head of the first one Ivan had used, and carefully replaced them in the box.

"I'm sorry." Ivan stood, embarrassed at losing his temper.

Silently, Cassie put the matches onto the shelf. Then she said, "Where do you really live?"

"I told you. Willowvale. Up near the ridge where we first met. Bruno Street. Near the high school. "

"Impossible. There are no houses there. It's outside the town walls. "

"Well, I live there. There are streets and houses and cars and all ordinary things. No horses and carts. No town wall. No curfews. Just ordinary."

"We need to talk. You are seriously weird. Help me finish these potatoes."

Ivan tried unsuccessfully to peel potatoes with a knife until Cassie said, "Just take the eyes out of them. I'll peel them." She put the full saucepan onto the stove and sat down to wait for the water to boil. Ivan stood uncomfortable, looking out of the window.

"I'm not stupid," he said quietly. "I'm sorry about the matches. I don't understand anything. That's all."

"You don't understand, and I don't know what to explain."

CHAPTER 5
OUTSIDE TOWN WALLS

"You can't look conspicuous. We don't want attention," said Thistle, who hid the worry Cassie attributed to her so well that Ivan couldn't see it at all. "Here, Ivan. Spare jacket. Wear it." They were in an unoccupied bedroom, and Thistle brought the mish-mash fur jacket hanging on a wire coat hanger out from a very ordinary-looking wardrobe. "We don't use it. Too small for me or Raven. Cassie doesn't need it. Warm." The skins that made up the jacket were from several animals. Ivan recognized grey-brown rabbit and red fox fur, and striped cat. Like the jacket Cassie wore, it was hung with tails. The fox's brush took place of honour in the centre of the back. The coat smelled like stuffed animals in a museum. "It's special. Look after it. Good for dancing too." Thistle spoke in spiky sentences, sharp as broken crockery. She watched as Ivan took his own jacket off and tried on the fur jacket, her eyes bright in the dim room. Ivan looked at himself in the mirror on the wardrobe door. He saw shadows and the reflection of light from the window, and himself a shaggy silhouette.

"I look wild!" he said, and laughed.

Thistle made an indistinct sound, half way between a laugh and a cough. "You look fine. Take these too." She gave Ivan a knitted hat and a hairy scarf. "You'll need them later. Cold. You can sleep here when we return." She swung her arm around the room in a stiff welcoming gesture. The bedroom contained the wardrobe, a bed piled with knitted and crocheted blankets, rugs made of fur, and patchwork quilts of crazy design. Sacks lumpy with vegetables, perhaps potatoes, leaned against the walls. There were wooden boxes with notes on them in charcoal: 'dried plums', 'apple leather'. An electrical cable dangled from the ceiling, no light bulb or shade. Instead a model of an eagle hung from it, cleverly made from carved sticks, string and feathers.

"Thank you."

Feeling a little too warm in the fur jacket, Ivan, with the others, was once more loaded with the leather bags that held the instruments from the hut outside town. Ivan was itching to try his hand at one of the instruments, but there was no time. Cassie and Thistle went ahead while Raven fed the dogs and checked that the ducks and goat had feed and water.

"It's better that we leave separately," Raven explained as he carefully locked the house.

"Why? And if the dance is not until tonight, why are we leaving so early? We've only just had lunch. And why is it such a big secret?"

Raven answered calmly. "Those who think they know what's best don't like music, dances, or, well, a number of things. They talk everywhere and would prevent us from going if they could. That's the first reason. The second is related to the first: we are going to be outside the town wall after the curfew. Some people only live by rules." Raven put the key into his pocket.

Ivan nodded to show that he understood and whistled for Frankie.

"Don't bring the dog, she's tired. She'll be too slow, and in the way. She'll be safe here with Magda and Wolfie."

Ivan would not be separated from Frankie. "She has to come." Ivan felt bad. He'd already had an argument with Cassie, and was about to start one with Raven. Frankie looked up at him. She seemed to smile trustingly. Ivan bent and stroked her soft ears. *I'll take you everywhere*, he promised with his eyes. Besides, he might have a chance to get back to the ridge at the power lines—or straight home—to get out of this world. He was sure that was the way home. He would never leave without Frankie. "She's coming," he said.

"Well then, she's your responsibility."

"Okay, fine."

Raven started for the back gate.

"Wait! I need a cord for her lead. I don't want her to run off."

Raven sighed. "Go back into Pip's room—into the front bedroom. There are cords in the top drawer in the wardrobe. Here's the back door key. Lock the house again on the way out." Ivan ran back, and in the drawer found a length of cord plaited from many coloured threads. It looked too beautiful to use for a dog's lead, but he was in a hurry, and Raven had said to use it. He locked the door and ran up the path to where Raven waited in the railway verge. Raven locked the back gate with a padlock while Ivan tied the cord onto Frankie's collar.

They walked by a back-street route through the town, crossed a branch of the creek by a footbridge upstream of a dammed pond that didn't exist in Ivan's world, and took more laneways and back streets until they reached the town wall. A path followed between back fences and the wall, which was built of pieces from all kinds of large objects—car bodies, broken up building materials, tree trunks and many other kinds of junk.

"We're nearly at the gate." Raven gestured to Ivan to stop, and watched carefully until nobody was nearby. "Follow me." He walked, not fast, toward a small doorway in the town wall, passed through and continued neither fast nor slowly toward a wide dirt road that Ivan recognized as the highway out of Willowvale. "That small gate is useful," said Raven quietly. "We'll only be on the high road for a short distance."

It was the middle of the afternoon and already the eccentric traffic of this place hurried home in its ramshackle way, heading for the main northern gateway. This was a large arched structure with a guard box and heavy gates of scrap iron. Ivan tried not to stare at the donkey carts and people carrying firewood on their backs and a large dog pulling a converted wheelbarrow, led by an old bent woman. Soon traffic was left behind as Raven turned into a deserted, ruined road that led uphill.

"It's quieter here," said Raven. They passed streets full of collapsed houses. Ivan wouldn't look at them. In all the overwhelming sights, experiences and smells of the town, he'd forgotten this strange, unsettling, deserted kind of place. The road of crumbled bitumen and potholes led, Ivan knew, toward the high school.

"You can ask questions when we reach the top of the hill," said Raven, as if he knew Ivan was about to open his mouth. It seemed it was going to be easier to get information from Raven than from the terse Thistle or from Cassie. Ivan began to look forward to the evening.

"Can Frankie have a rest?" The dog was dragging behind on her lead.

"No, carry her."

It was strange how long the hill seemed. The leather bags bumped and rubbed on Ivan's back, making muffled musical sounds. Frankie was heavy. This road was one Ivan often travelled in his own life. Now he realized it was usually in the luxury of a car or walking with his friends, talking and distracted. The centre of town inside the walls was so different from normal that it hardly seemed the same place—but here, despite the ruins and potholes, things were in a weird way familiar. The line of deciduous trees that shaded the footpath in summer was there, and ghostly side streets branched off in the right places.

They reached the top of the hill where Ivan knew the road

would lead down a straight stretch to the school—and toward his house, which was only a block from school. Right now Mum would be asking Reenie and Anna how their day was, and telling them not to leave their school bags in the middle of the hallway…no, she wouldn't. They'd all be worrying about him…

"Anyone we're likely to meet from here on is a friend," said Raven. "Ask me your questions. I know you have many."

Ivan opened his mouth and shut it, not knowing what to ask. There were indeed so many questions. Would Raven answer any, every one? Or would he refuse, say they were foolish questions? "What's the curfew? Why?" Ivan's was surprised by his own question. There were more important things to find out, but it was asked now.

Raven looked surprised too. "It's a signal to get inside the town walls." He started to walk down the road toward the school.

"The drums?"

"Yes, they're the signal."

"What is the danger? Why is it dangerous?"

"There are many dangers—real ones—and—how can I say it…imaginary ones as well."

"And?"

"And what?"

"What are these dangers?"

"The animals. Outsiders. Ferals. Natural disasters."

"Which of those are real?"

"Cassie says you've seen one of the animals," said Raven vaguely.

Ivan had seen many things in the last twenty-four hours. The animal was strange but not the most incomprehensible. The hairs on his arms stood up as he remembered the crashing in the bush as he leapt off the flying fox platform, and the large creature that he glimpsed. "A wombat? Maybe a big one. A bear? There are no bears in this country. A Diprotodon? They don't even exist. My imagination's running away with me." He realized that he was talking to himself.

Raven had stopped to speak to some people who appeared from a side street. Ivan waited. The conversation seemed absorbing, and the group walked slowly. Ivan was tired of meeting people, and of their reactions to him. He put Frankie down and walked on, not fast, not slow.

It was almost possible here—where in both this town and in Ivan's version of the town, the road was fringed with trees—to imagine he'd be home soon. The school buildings were an untidy village of their own, grouped around the hall. They looked less ruined than other buildings outside the town walls—or was the lowering afternoon light playing tricks? Ivan looked back. Raven walked with several other people now. The musical instruments bumped on Ivan's hip and the straps of their bags pulled at his neck and shoulder. Over near the hall where yesterday Ivan had been lining up for school assembly, figures were moving. It looked so ordinary. Across the road and up one block was Ivan's house. He wanted to go there, but his feet carried him to the hall.

The main side door was open. Ivan went in. It was almost like a school social with the theme 'Ferals'. Ivan laughed out loud at the thought—then felt cold as he caught his own thoughts tricking him into thinking things could be normal here. And Raven had said that ferals were one of the real—or were they imaginary dangers? Was this a trick? Most of the people here made Raven, Thistle and Cassie's appearance seem positively conventional.

Ivan paused at the door. A woman sat behind an old school exam desk. "Ah, Thistle and Raven's friend. You'll have to leave the dog outside, dear. Tie it up near the door. Funny little thing, isn't it?"

Yes, Ivan thought, the dogs here all looked purposeful, working dogs. Frankie was definitely different. He took her outside and tied the cord lead to a railing, and returned to the woman at the desk.

"Take the instruments over there." She pointed into the main hall. Ivan hesitated. "Just in through the door. Thistle's expecting you. Go on."

The hall was scattered with groups of people talking and laughing, dressed in a mixture of old and home-made, like the people in town, but to a completely different result. Old evening clothes thrown together in peculiar ways and wild hairstyles strongly favouring dreadlocks and wreaths of foliage gave the room a festive appearance that was absent from the town. Children of all sizes from toddlers up ran and shouted between the adults. He saw Thistle. She was dressed in her usual baggy trousers, but with several layers of brightly coloured shirts on top tied across the chest with silk scarves. She had set up a large table in front of the stage, and on it were arranged the musical instruments, unwrapped at last. Polished wooden shapes with strings and slender necks. Strange flutes. Small harps. Even a trumpet-like creation incorporating a ram's horn. They were beautiful. Ivan wanted to try all of them. Thistle was immersed in conversation with a bearded man in an ancient army greatcoat and a feather boa. It was the first time Ivan had seen her smile. People crowded around the table, touching, trying notes on the instruments.

The dusty blue velvet stage curtains were half drawn. Ivan saw Cassie on the stage moving chairs around talking to a skinny boy who arranged rickety music stands and an older girl with long dreadlocks wearing a red satin evening dress and a woollen lumberjack's coat. Cassie was dressed in an ancient evening dress of green velvet. She looked very different, and the effect was not entirely spoiled by her heavy leather boots and hand-knitted socks.

Nobody paid any attention to Ivan. The cat-fox-rabbit jacket definitely had the desired effect here. He worked his way to Thistle's table and placed the bags on the floor behind it. Thistle smiled at him. He nodded to her and fitted himself between people, back to the main floor.

Ivan's heart beat fast. He was so close to his home, only a block away. He could almost see Mum waiting by the phone for the police to call, Anna watching her anxiously, her favourite TV show flickering unwatched in the lounge room—Dad and Reenie out searching the bush—Gran and Pop—the real Gran and Pop—at home with the phone book, ringing everyone they could think of. He must go to them.

Raven and his friends would arrive soon. He would forbid Ivan to be outside so close to the curfew. There was a door on the far side of the hall, a fire escape. Ivan sauntered across to it and experimentally pushed at the catch. The door creaked open and he slipped out through a small gap, closing the door carefully. Frankie watched the other door. Ivan waited at the corner of the building while a few people entered, then ran to her, untied the cord from the railing and sprinted across the road and into a side street. Long shadows streaked from every tree. *Not much time.* Ivan was sure there was something significant about sunset.

Raven and his friends were near the hall now. Mick was one of them, and people who looked a lot like Mrs Thompson and Aunty Sue. Ivan forced himself to take his eyes from them. He clicked his tongue quietly to Frankie and, head down, ran toward home.

The closer Ivan was to home, the more difficult it was to keep going. He knew every slab of cement on the footpath, every fence, every tree, even the layout of back yards he cut through to save time. Enough was the same—he knew where he was. But the ruins and weeds, the overgrown piles of rubble, car skeletons and power poles swinging dead wires, were a fearsome defence to be passed, in his mind if not in reality. The closer he was to home, the more Ivan knew that it was going to be exactly the same as all the other houses—just a depressing ghost of something that had no existence in this world.

I can't do this. Ivan sat down on the ground. He felt weak.

Frankie put her front paws on his knee and licked his face. She knew where she was. She pulled on the cord lead, whining. Ivan got up and let her pull him along. He could see from her behaviour that Frankie was both excited and scared.

CHAPTER 6
CAL

Reenie stared down from the lookout rock. She didn't see the view of distant hills or the houses at the bottom of the valley. She didn't want to see them. She wanted to see Ivan. It almost physically hurt, her wish that he would walk round the bend of the track, and ask why she was standing there looking so dismal, as if everything was normal. Maybe he'd even start an argument in his annoying younger-brother way. That would be wonderful.

The path and rocks were the same as they'd always been…until yesterday. Now the scene was cold and mysterious instead of comfortable. She looked at the sloping rock where she'd found Ivan's book yesterday. There was the clear dusty ground where his footprints were trodden by others, and the small paw prints of Frankie still circling the edges of the dust where people hadn't walked. Nothing would be right until he came back. She looked away, focused her eyes on nothing, or on infinity. *Where is he?* Reenie asked God or the hills or the sky. The hills and sky remained grey. They seemed to move away from her as she stared at them, making Reenie feel dizzy. God didn't speak. She walked to the place where she'd found Ivan's book and looked down, scrutinising the lichen on the rock as if she could read it.

A small wind lifted the leaves of the gum trees and rubbed branches together with an eerie creaking sound. Down in the valley someone started to practise on a drum kit. Reenie brushed the blowing hair away from her face and turned for home.

"Oh—I didn't see you." A new boy from school—Reenie didn't know his name—stood by the base of the power poles, his face very still. "Are you okay?" asked Reenie. The boy looked bleak.

"Hear that? The drums?"

"Are you one of Ivan's friends?"

"I don't know." The boy held his hand up to silence her. "They've stopped." He looked down the span of the power lines. "Too early."

"If you're not Ivan's friend why are you here?"

"Who are you talking about?" interrupted the boy.

"My brother Ivan."

"Ivan?"

"Ivan Williams. Longish brown hair, blue eyes, skinny, plays the guitar—" Reenie remembered Ivan saying something about music being one of the reasons he was bullied. "Plays music. He's good at it."

"Oh, him."

The throwaway dismissal of the boy's voice made Reenie look more closely at him. She took a sharp breath. "Are you the one that hates him? Picks on him?"

"No. Yes. I don't know." The boy spoke distantly, as if he was distracted by something more urgent that took his attention from the conversation.

"I have to go. Mum's going to be worried."

"Why? It's early, too early."

Reenie sighed and turned away.

"Wait. You're right. It was me. Tell Ivan I didn't mean—you're wrong—I don't hate him…stay and talk."

"Mum's really jumpy since Ivan's gone missing—wouldn't you be if you were her? I have to go."

"Gone missing?" For the first time the boy's full attention turned on Reenie.

"Do you live under a rock? He disappeared last night. We haven't seen him since he came home from school yesterday and went straight out again. Didn't you know? It's been all over school."

"Well...no..." he looked down and across at her, then appeared to change his mind about what he was going to say. "I've been away..."

Reenie thought he was lying. "Why are you here if you're not helping search for Ivan?" The ridge had been criss-crossed over and over by police, volunteers, and family and friends all day. It was amazing that none of them were crashing in the bush nearby now. She started backing toward the track that led to home. There was something unnerving about the boy.

The boy turned to follow her movement with his eyes. "I come here because it reminds me of home. I lost something here once, I need to find it. I don't know." He spoke in fragments of sentences, his speech like a phone call breaking up. He put his hand into his jeans pocket, found nothing. "You'd better go."

Reenie wanted to go.

The boy looked out over the valley, his hair curling off his head like dark flames. His face was as desolate as Reenie felt.

"What's your name?" she asked.

"Call me..." the boy studied Reenie for a long moment. "Call me Cal." He shivered and swung a jacket over his shoulders. A black leather jacket dripping with buckles, straps and strangely shaped studs.

Reenie jolted back into conversation when she saw the jacket. Ivan had said something about a boy with an unusual jacket. She felt like a malfunctioning phone, herself. "Oh. You really are the one. So you're sorry for the way you treated Ivan? How can I believe you?"

"Yeah. I am sorry."

"Well, if he ever comes back, I'll tell him. It's probably your fault that he ran away."

"Why are you up here?" asked Cal.

"I found Ivan's book here. I thought he might come back. To this place."

"Where? Show me." Cal almost flew over the rocks to Reenie. He grabbed her hand in his cold, dry one. She stepped back in fright. "Sorry. Can you show me?"

"Where's the place this reminds you of?"

"Doesn't matter. Can you show me where you found the book? Please."

"I've got to go. Mum will be freaking out." Reenie didn't recognize Cal's name. She'd never met him before, but he must be the person who made Ivan's life miserable. Why would he say he was, if it wasn't true? The new boy Ivan had come home talking about, the boy with the cool leather jacket, the boy who just appeared from nowhere. The one about whom shortly afterwards Ivan wouldn't talk at all, except to grunt evasively.

"I thought you were called something else," said Reenie, trying to remember whether Ivan had ever mentioned his name. Her curiosity was keeping Mum waiting, she thought, but she had to ask.

"Oh. Yeah. I've got lots of names. Call me anything. Cal's my real name. You understand? I don't tell everyone my real name."

She should hate him, but she felt sorry for him. "The book was right here." She pointed.

Cal looked at the rock as closely as Reenie had looked at it, as if he, too, could read the mineral crystals, the cracks, the lichen. "So he did go there, then. I thought he just ducked down over the rocks. It should have been me." His face set in an expression that was a mixture of quiet anger and despair.

"What do you mean?"

"Oh, nothing." Suddenly Cal took Reenie by both shoulders and looked into her eyes. "When—if—when he comes back, it'll be to here that he'll come. Here. And if you notice that I'm gone, any time, any time...be happy for me. Don't worry about me. Promise?"

"I really, really have to go," stammered Reenie, tears of pity, fear, and frustration forming in her eyes. "Don't do anything stupid, Cal."

Cal let his hands fall from her shoulders and turned to look over the valley again. "I'm through with doing stupid stuff. When you see Ivan, tell him I'm sorry."

CHAPTER 7
THE RIDGE AT SUNSET

Frankie whined. As Ivan feared, there was nothing but the garden reclaimed by nature, some old cement paths, brick foundations and the big eucalyptus tree that always towered over the house.

Ivan walked through the place where the front gate wasn't, up the cracked cement path between grasping weeds and grass and colonizing wattle trees that were never there before. The front steps led up to—up to nothing. Ignoring this fact Ivan stepped onto the rubbly ground that was in place of the hallway beyond the front door.

"I'm home!" he called. "Hey, Mum, Dad, I'm back. Reenie, Anna, are you there?" In his mind he saw the house materialize around him. Walls appeared; the old carpet that his parents sometimes spoke of replacing grew across the floor like a lawn, Reenie's and his own school books and Anna's toys scattered themselves over it. The smell of lamb chops cooking floated from the kitchen and he heard the radio's faint voice.

He heard, saw, smelt nothing—it was all imagination. Ivan's hand was extended in expectation of feeling the textured wallpaper that had been in the house since it was built. Like Gran and Pop, Mum and Dad were not inclined toward unnecessary home renovations.

Nothing. Just cold air and a weed that stroked its spines along his fingers. "Mum? Dad? Anna, Reen…" Ivan's voice fell flat on the empty foundations. Frankie shivered so suddenly and dramatically that he felt the loop of her lead shake on his wrist. The last vestige of home snapped off like a light turned out. Ivan stood among the ruins of a place that he didn't really recognize.

The sun was balanced on the treetops at the ridge. Ivan's thoughts focused on the image. The power lines. The special place. I'll be there as the drums sound, like I was yesterday. Maybe that's the key.

Stumbling over debris, Ivan ran up the road and into the bush reserve. The fire trails were overgrown, but he knew the place—he saw boulders and ancient fallen trees that were like old friends who kept unchanged amid upheaval.

Cold breath ripped through Ivan's lungs. Frankie's lead fell from his numb fingers and she panted behind him, trailing the piece of cord. His leg muscles burned. Icy air needled down his windpipe. His foot slipped off a rock, grazing his anklebone. Ivan paused to rub it and catch his breath. He could see the top of the ridge—the place where the track should branch to the flat rock and the power poles and the electrical wires that swooped down to the valley and out of town.

Now Frankie rushed ahead of him, drawn on by mysterious canine excitement. Ivan followed, limping. He saw the ridge top flatten and the sun perched on treetops across the valley sending cold rays sifting through the gum leaves. He couldn't get enough air into his chest. The narrow track that should lead to the power poles disappeared between grevillea shrubs and spiny bursaria bushes. Ivan tore through them ignoring scratches and stabs and the cuts of knife-hard grasses.

The poles came into view, and the platform for leaping and the large rock where Ivan sat to read in his own world. He almost fell through the grevilleas as faintly the drums began. Frankie was at the base of the poles. Ivan was halfway to the flat rock when she barked sharply. The drum signal intensified. There was the place he'd left his book on the rock yesterday, though it seemed like half a lifetime ago. Ivan wanted to get there, to the place where he had been—desperately. Frankie yelped again. The urgent beat of the drums swelled and filled Ivan's head painfully. He hurried through the darkening bushes toward the dog.

Frankie was there—and then she wasn't. One moment her small shape was silhouetted by the last sunlight, and the next moment the space she had occupied was empty.

Ivan ran forward. "Frankie! Wait!" He stood on the place where she had stood, and waited while the drums faded to silence. Maybe they were both home now, in the bush that led to his house and family.

"Frankie! Come here." He whistled. No sound of Frankie anywhere. The air cooled now that the sun was gone. Ivan thrust his hands into the fur jacket's pockets to warm them. He started to walk toward home, just in case he was in his own world now and Frankie was ahead of him, but he didn't really think he was in the right Willowvale. He felt a stab of homesickness. Ivan pulled the jacket close across his chest. Something red on the grey ground caught his eye—a battered Swiss army knife. Ivan picked it up. The red plastic casing had fallen off one side of the knife. He levered it open. The blade was fine steel, and had been sharpened many times.

Suddenly there was a movement in the bushes behind Ivan. He turned.

An animal crouched there. It was the one Ivan had seen yesterday. Not letting his eyes leave the animal, holding the small knife up like a dagger, he began to back away. The animal growled low in its throat. What was it? Ivan clutched the knife in his right hand though he knew that the short blade was no defence if the animal attacked.

Time slowed. Suddenly Ivan's mind switched to top gear. More than anything the animal resembled an overgrown wombat. Wombats aren't particularly dangerous—unless you go into their burrows. Ivan tried to convince himself it was just a wombat. The animal's growl rumbled to nothing. It stayed in the bushes, not attempting to approach or attack. Ivan knew he'd heard the drums fade to echoes that hung in the air like smoke. It was too late today. Frankie had gone home, and he was still stuck here. The sun was a cold glow behind the higher hills across the valley.

The wombat lunged toward him. Ivan broke away and spun around, galloping down the ridge the way he'd come. Wombats may not be dangerous, but they can be fast and aggressive if they choose, he remembered. And they have strong teeth and claws.

Ivan sprinted down the hillside. Everything was a blur of too many shapes—leaves, sticks, rocks, lichen. He couldn't tell if the animal was chasing after him or not; his own noise was enough for both of them. Ivan's grazed ankle and all the other little injuries of the last twenty-four hours hurt, but he kept running, sure he could hear the wombat crashing through the bush after him. At last near the first wrecked street that led down to the school, Ivan paused for breath. There was no sound of pursuit. Surely the animal wouldn't follow into the streets. Ivan jogged on down the hill, gasping icy air that tore at his throat. It was only a few blocks to the school. He skidded around a corner into Oliver Street and saw a campfire in a brick chimney that stood alone where once had been a house.

"Who's that?" called a rough voice.

It was too late to hide in silence after his tumbling descent of the hillside. Ivan stood still.

"Who's there?" repeated the voice loudly. "Show yourself. We know you're there." Footsteps crunched across sticks. A large figure strode toward Ivan, holding a heavy wooden staff.

"John—careful." A woman's voice. A baby cried out and stopped.

"Who? Show yourself." The man called John lifted the staff above his head, his eyes dazzled by firelight, though it wasn't yet completely dark.

Ivan stepped forward. "Who are you?"

The man saw Ivan—he lowered his staff and took a step back. He was not tall, but solidly built. His bulky coat made him look squarer. "Just a boy," he said, as if to himself. His eyes, adjusting to the light, felt their way over Ivan in a careful inspection. "What are you doing here, boy?"

"I'm going to a dance." Ivan realized how silly that sounded as he said it.

"Who are you? I don't know you. And what's that animal?" Ivan's heart jumped. Animal? He looked behind him for the wombat. "That fur thing."

Ivan was confused. Was the wombat behind him? *No.*

John pointed at his chest with the stick.

"Oh. It's only a coat made of skins."

"John, John," called the woman, "be careful."

"Who are you then, and where'd you steal this coat from? I don't know you."

"I'm just going to the dance."

"Is he dangerous?" called the woman's voice. Her fearful tone communicated to the baby, who began a weak wailing cry.

"Just a boy," said John.

"I'm going to the dance," said Ivan for the third time. "I don't want to bother you."

"Are you from Willowvale?" The man sounded puzzled.

"Yes—" the man took a threatening step forward at this— "No—I'm—I don't know."

"Come on, tell the truth, boy."

"I'm staying with Raven and Thistle. I'm going to their dance."

It was nearly dark now, but Ivan saw John relax his stance. "Oh, well, I suppose if you know them—" he turned and called to the woman, "A friend, Jules, a friend of Thistle and Raven's. To Ivan he said, "You shouldn't be wandering around. Do Raven and Thistle know you're out here? How about that girl of theirs? She with you?"

"Ask him over," called the woman, her voice friendly now.

"I have to get back," said Ivan.

"Just say hello," said John. "Jules doesn't see many people." Ivan didn't like to refuse. He and John crossed to the fire. The woman sat on a log. Her baby cried snufflingly. She bent over it under her blanket cloak and the cries calmed.

"Hello," said Ivan.

"Who are you?"

"Ivan—Williams."

"Williams, eh? Related to them in town?"

"Yes—no—I think so—"

"He doesn't know much," commented John.

"I'm Ju-li-a" said the woman slowly, as if she thought Ivan was of limited intelligence. "This is John. The baby's name is Isabel."

"Nice to meet you," said Ivan.

"Going to the dance, eh?"

"Yes, I have to get back there, I'm in a bit of a hurry."

"Wandering round the bush after the drums…why? It's not allowed, you should know that."

Ivan didn't answer.

"See anything?" she asked sharply.

"Not much," said Ivan warily.

"I'll take him down to the dance," said John.

"Don't be long, John."

"Come on, Ivan Williams," said John. They walked along the cracked footpaths. It wasn't far to the school.

"I know the way."

"Yeah—but you don't know much else. The curfew, for instance."

"I had something to do. It was important."

"Oh, right," said John sarcastically. "Who are you really?" His voice took on a menacing edge again. "Ivan—never heard of an Ivan before inside or out the walls. Williams? Williams? I've seen all the Williamses and none of them are you. Mick, Penny, Michelle, Cathy, Jack, old Mr and Mrs Williams…" Ivan felt John's eyes search over him in the dimness. "And yet—I've seen that jacket before—Raven and Thistle, eh? I want to see them and talk to them for myself."

"What do you mean?"

"How do I know you're not an outsider?"

"What are you? You live outside."

"Don't insult me, boy. I'm a feral, not an outsider. You could be one, come from past the pit with your whim-whams and gizmos…" His voice faded into an incoherent muddle of words.

Ivan tried to make more distance between himself and John. Suddenly he realized that he still held the open pocketknife in his other hand.

John was watching, and saw the blade glint. "Got a knife, have you? I knew it. Give it here."

Ivan snapped the knife shut, and tried to put it into the jacket pocket.

John moved like lightning, grabbed his wrist in an iron grip. "Let me have that knife." He twisted it out of Ivan's grasp and held it close to his eyes. He ran his finger over the plastic casing. "This isn't yours. This is Pip's knife. I can feel his name where he carved it. Raven and Thistle have been searching for clues for a year. Where'd you get it?" His large hand closed more tightly on Ivan's wrist and he strode down the hill so fast that Ivan stumbled, keeping up.

"You're in big trouble, Mister Ivan—ha—Williams—I don't think," muttered John. "And now that I think of it, that's Pip's jacket too. Thistle would never lend that to someone like you in a million years." He increased his pace. Ivan could barely stay on his feet.

No lights showed at the hall but as they came near the sound of thumping feet and reedy music filtered out through the closed doors. John changed his grasp to Ivan's elbow and dragged him up the steps. He crashed through the door, past the friendly woman at the desk, whose mouth fell open in what would have been a comical expression if it had been a funny situation, and pulled Ivan into the candle-lit hall.

"Raven! Do you know anything about this boy?" yelled John so loudly that his voice rang over the music and patterns of footfalls on the wooden floor. The band faltered raggedly to silence and every face turned to look at John and Ivan.

Raven, Thistle and Cassie were on the stage among the musicians, already on their feet. John shook Ivan like a dog shaking a bone.

"It's all right, John," shouted Raven. "He's with us."

John let go Ivan's arm. Ivan fell to the floor and stayed there, shaking with anger and fright.

"I found him up the ridge. He's stolen Pip's jacket and knife. How do you know he's not an outsider spy? He nearly frightened Jules and the baby out of their wits."

Raven was halfway to John and Ivan now, closely followed by Thistle. Cassie stood among the musicians, her face white, her instrument in her hand.

"It's all right," repeated Raven. He put a hand on John's arm. Thistle, her mouth clamped in a straight line, ran to Ivan and helped him up.

"I thought you were all coming to the dance, John," said Raven.

John went red with what appeared to be embarrassment. "Isabel's got a cold. Jules didn't want to come. Can't be too careful these days," he muttered, "especially when I saw Pip's things. His coat. His knife." He shook Raven's hand off his arm. "You're too trusting, Raven."

"I'll have Pip's knife, thanks, John," said Raven. John handed the knife to him and left the hall without another word. Cassie jumped from the stage and took the knife from Raven's hand—he didn't notice, watching John leave in abstracted silence.

Ivan watched him go while around him the dancers reformed their sets. The musicians struck up a bright jiggy tune. Cassie stood among the dancers, still white-faced while Raven and Thistle took Ivan to their trading table.

"You sit quietly here," said Thistle, not unkindly. She and Raven returned to their places in the band. Someone put a mug of vegetable soup in front of Ivan but all he could do was shiver. His ankle hurt, his wrist and elbow still bore the print of John's fingers and his shoulder still ached from the wrenching on the flying fox. The dancers formed rings and spun around faster and faster. The music matched their actions, round and round.

"Ivan. Dance with me." Cassie interrupted Ivan's mug of soup with a shake of the shoulder. "I'm not playing this dance."

"I can't dance."

"I'll teach you. It's easy."

After years of school socials in this hall not knowing what to do and hoping it would be time to go home soon, Ivan found himself having a good time. Cassie pushed him round a fast dance, which he gradually came to understand. The dizziness from the dancing overtook his tiredness and he gave himself over to enjoyment.

CHAPTER 8
CAL COMES TO DINNER

Reenie knew she had to get home. She watched as Cal walked away. Cal's flaming hair moved among the grey tree trunks. It was the only bright thing about him. Somehow he made Reenie feel sadder. His mood bled into hers.

Reenie shook herself and began to hurry along the track. *Got to get home. Force yourself to think of how Cal tormented Ivan, how he must have said horrible things to him, made fun of him for the things he loved—loves—don't be sorry for Cal.* But she did feel sorry for him. He communicated controlled desperation and a sadness that soaked into her like water through limestone, mixing with her worry about Ivan.

Where was he? People don't just disappear for no reason. Sorrow rose inside her. Tears formed in her eyes. So much sadness everywhere. Reenie thought of Frankie. Tears rolled down her face as she walked, and through misty vision she imagined she saw the dog trotting around, sniffing the ground, coming close for a pat then circling around a tree. *Why am I crying for the dog, and not for Ivan*, Reenie thought, and realized that she was crying for Ivan. She rounded a bend, wiping her eyes with the back of her hand.

The track divided here. One fork led to the streets below the ridge. The other meandered off into the bush. Reenie peered down the main track, expecting to see Cal ahead of her, but she could not see him. She turned on the spot, scanning the bush. Not that he was likely to be in trouble or anything, but it was puzzling that he had disappeared. Just then she saw a movement on the side track. Cal's red hair moved in and out of sight. Reenie ran after him, not quite knowing why. It was important, that's all. "Cal—wait—where are you going?"

"Home."

"There are no houses there."

Cal shrugged.

"Where do you live?" Reenie swiped her hand across her face and sniffed.

"Around here. About."

"Are you all right?"

"Yeah, yeah."

Reenie looked down at the ground and sniffed again. "I was going to ask you—come to our place for dinner?"

Cal's eyebrows rose. Reenie felt surprised too.

"Why?"

Reenie felt her face flush. But she'd been crying, so it probably didn't show. Oh arggh…"Just thought—thought you might be, um, hungry." Cal was very thin. His eyebrows stayed way up his forehead, and a shadow of a smile passed over his face.

"Won't your parents be busy? You said yourself they're frantic. They won't want me hanging around. And I'm not exactly Ivan's best friend, they probably hate my guts. Like you seem to—" His smile flickered and disappeared. "And I wouldn't blame them."

"They don't know about that. Ivan never said anything about you. It'll be a distraction for them. Gran's around, she always cooks too much."

Cal shrugged again. A currawong called, and through the dusk came sounds of cars in the streets below, and dogs barking.

Reenie thought she heard drums float faintly down over the top of the ridge.

Cal tensed, and for a moment she thought he was going to run away from her and back up the hill for a reason that she could not understand, but he smiled. "I'd love to come."

There had been no rest for Mum or Dad since Ivan's disappearance. Reenie could see from a distance that the car was gone, meaning Mum was out after all. She was probably driving round the district or wandering the bush or down at the police station asking and answering questions. Dad was at work, or out doing the same as Mum. She hadn't seen a lot of them since the panicked, horror-struck moments when they realized Ivan wasn't coming home, only the odd times they stumbled home to drink cups of tea and eat Gran's lamb chops and mashed potato without tasting them. When they were home, they were like shadows, watching Reenie and Anna every moment, as if they too would disappear into thin air. Thank God for Gran and Pop. *They must be just as terrified as the rest of us, but they're holding everyone else up with all their strength.* Reenie shut her mouth to prevent a sob coming out and pushed on down the hill.

The screen door closed with a slam. Reenie stepped over the school bags in the hall. Ivan's was still there where he'd dropped it.

"Hello, dear," called Gran from the dining room. Reenie could see her sitting at the table with Anna, no doubt keeping a constant ear on the phone. There was a board and a pile of vegetables on the table. The TV was on, but Anna was sitting with her back to it, with coloured pens and pieces of paper scattered in front of her, drawing a picture which Reenie feared was probably of Ivan.

"Hi Gran. I've got a friend—"

"Bring her in and introduce her then."

Cal looked alarmed. He jerked his head toward the door, as if he would leave immediately. Reenie grabbed his wrist before he could touch the door handle, and led him down the hall. Gran looked worn and pale.

"Are you okay, Gran?" said Reenie.

"Nothing to worry about, dear. I'm just overwrought, like everyone. I could have sworn I heard Ivan walk in the door a few minutes ago, but it was my imagination. Now, who's your friend?"

"This is—" she remembered that Cal didn't tell everyone his real name, and faltered.

"Everyone calls me Phil," said Cal quietly.

Unfortunately, as they entered the dining room, Reenie forgot she was still holding Cal by the wrist and in her concern for Gran had forgotten to let go. Gran's attention was on the beans she was slicing, but Anna, who had been watching silently up to this point, shrieked, "Reenie's got a boyfriend!" Reenie and Cal snatched their hands back.

Gran said sharply to Anna, "Don't be silly." She looked up. "Who is this, then, dear?"

"This is Phil, he goes to school," said Reenie. It sounded stupid, but she couldn't think of anything else to say.

"Hello, Phil, it's nice to meet you."

"Hello…um, Mrs Williams," said Cal.

"Can…Phil stay to dinner?"

Gran paused for a moment, perhaps calculating how much food she had. "If it's all right with his parents…" Her voice trailed off as she looked away from the beans and took in Cal's appearance. He didn't look like someone the location of whom his parents were always aware. He didn't look much like someone who even had parents.

"They won't mind," said Cal quickly.

"Are you really Reenie's boyfriend?" asked Anna.

"No, he's not, shut up."

"Reenie, that's a nice name, is it short for something?" said Cal, and Reenie realized she hadn't told him her name.

"Irini. Mum's parents are Russian. It's a family name."

"You'd better ring your parents, Phil," said Gran. "I'd feel easier, under the circumstances."

"I can't, I don't have a mobile."

"You can ring from our phone. I'll show you where it is."

Reenie showed Cal the phone, in the kitchen. She poured glasses of juice while Cal fiddled with the buttons on the phone, then said abruptly into it, "Hello, this is, it's me—I'm at Reenie's place for dinner, I'll be late." He turned and Reenie, watching over the rim of her glass, saw that his face had that bleak look again, as if he'd been cold for too long, pale and pinched. "Bye," he said, and put the phone receiver down on the kitchen bench, forgetting to hang up the phone.

"Have a juice," said Reenie. Cal's hand shook as he picked up the glass. "Are you sure you're okay?" Absently Reenie picked up the phone receiver and hung it on the phone, almost expecting to hear Cal's mother's voice asking for details. She could imagine Mum or Dad if she rang them like that. We don't know them do we? Where do they live? What time shall we pick you up, about eight? Don't forget you have homework…but then Cal really didn't look like a child of parents like hers.

Cal drained his glass. Gran gathered up the vegetables in two saucepans and came into the kitchen. "Out, you're in the way," she said. "Make yourselves useful, and bring in some firewood. Your dad won't have time, take some of the weight off his shoulders, Reenie, dear."

Dinner was on the table. Gran's "good plain food", as Pop always called it. Pop had arrived in time to kiss the girls, meet Cal and thump himself down at the table in the seat that faced the TV news. Reenie looked at her plate. She was hungry but not hungry. She felt cold despite the fire that glowed in the fireplace across the sitting room. Cal had found a place in Gran's heart by bringing in a huge pile of logs, and now sat before a plate piled high with mashed potato, beans, carrots and chops. Anna ate without paying attention to her food, eyes on Cal. Reenie knew that despite the horrible fact of Ivan's absence and all the disruption, Anna's mind was seething with pointless ten-year-old's questions relating to Cal and herself. Cal ate hungrily, though, like Anna, not watching his food. His eyes were on Gran, and Pop, his face as full of questions as Anna's.

"Eat up, love," said Gran to no-one in particular, and to all of them, "you need it."

"Will Mum and Dad be home soon?" said Anna.

"Don't worry," said Pop, "they'll be here soon." As he spoke, a car entered the driveway.

Anna jumped up. "It's them! Maybe they've found him!" She rushed from the room, her feet thumping on the hall floor, and flung the front door open. Gran got up too, and went to the kitchen to fetch the two plates kept warm in the oven.

"Reenie! Gran! Pop! Come here!" Anna's voice was urgent. Reenie jumped up so quickly that her chair fell flat on the floor behind her, and ran after Anna. Gran and Pop followed. Cal stayed uncertainly at the table.

Reenie ran along the hallway, out through the front door and jumped down the steps in one leap. Ivan must have come home! She felt a laugh of excitement form in her throat and heard her voice call out, "Ivan!"

Where is he? And where are Mum, Dad and Anna? The car was in the driveway, lights still blazing. She couldn't see them in the dark.

"I can't believe it," Dad said heavily from the darkness.

Mum stood up from behind the car. "Well, it's better than nothing," she said quietly. Reenie was surprised. What did they mean?

"Reenie! She's back!" Anna came out of the dark toward Reenie. She held Frankie in her arms.

Reenie stood still. "Not Ivan?" Her laugh became a sob and stuck in her throat as it changed. Abruptly she turned and ran inside, pushing past Gran and Pop as they emerged from the house.

Cal was still in the dining room. Reenie couldn't reach the privacy of her own room without passing him.

"What's wrong?"

Reenie covered her face and sobbed, gasping for breath and self-control. She tried to push past Cal the way she had past her grandparents, but he grabbed her arm and stopped her.

"It's just Frankie, not Ivan—only the dog."

"Are you all right?"

"I wanted it to be Ivan. I thought—"

Cal steered her to a chair. She put her head down on the table and tried to calm herself. The rest of the family were coming.

"I should go. I'm in the way," said Cal. Reenie looked up. He had that alone look again, the one that had faded a little in the last half hour.

It was too late for Cal to slip away politely. Anna burst in carrying Frankie, drawing Mum, Dad, Gran and Pop in her wake. Cal bent near Reenie. "I'd better go," he said, and she almost thought he was going to kiss the top of her head the way adults kiss small children. On top of the other emotions that were storming around inside her, Reenie felt her breath jump.

Anna hugged Frankie tightly to her chest. Frankie squirmed in her arms, trying to lick her face. Mum and Dad stared in a surprised manner at Cal.

"Hello, um, I'm a friend of Reenie's, I was just leaving, it's not a good time..." His voice trailed away to nothing, his eyes jumping from Reenie's father to the dog and back again.

"Suit yourself," said Dad, too tired for politeness. He threw his car keys down on the bench that cut through from the dining room to the kitchen and sat down at the table. "Elena and I didn't find anything today," he said to Gran and Pop. Cal didn't seem offended, but continued to stare from him to Frankie and back, mouth slightly open.

"The boy might as well finish his tea," said Gran. Cal said nothing and sat down heavily as Dad had, still staring.

Reenie drew a breath and wiped the back of her hand across her face.

"Tissue, dear," said Gran.

"You're Mick Williams," said Cal suddenly. Mick didn't seem to hear. "But you can't be..."

Mick looked at him. He had heard. "I don't know you, sonny, but lots of people know me, and I'm definitely one of a kind. I assure you I am me." He turned his attention to his food.

Cal's face went bright red with embarrassment. He ate the rest of his dinner quickly, leaving nothing but clean bones on his plate, not looking at anyone, his eyes fixed with intense interest on the dog to avoid having to talk, Reenie guessed. Frankie sat at Anna's feet, gobbling the titbits Anna surreptitiously dropped from her plate.

Soon Cal stood and picked up his plate and glass. "I have to go. Thanks for having me," he said.

Reenie was as embarrassed by the situation as Cal. She too stood up. "I'll walk you to the door," she said.

"Feed the dog, Reenie, would you, while you're up," said Mum tiredly.

Reenie called Frankie. Cal followed her into the kitchen. She took a can of dog food from the fridge. "I feed her out the back; you might as well go out that way with me."

"You feed the dog out of a can?" Cal said, as if he wasn't thinking, then looked as if he wished he had not said it when he saw Reenie's puzzled expression.

They walked through the living room where even Anna was now silent and solemn. Cal was silent too, but seemed to be full of a mysterious excitement. They went out onto the back steps. Cal scooped Frankie up while Reenie spooned dog food out of the can.

Cal held Frankie close to his face. "You came tonight?" he said to her.

Frankie tried to lick his nose.

"I know you've been there. It should have been me, going back. How could I miss it? It's my own fault."

"She's probably only been up the bush, chasing wombats," said Reenie. "What makes you think she's been…wherever you think she's been? She has run away before. Lots of times."

"She was with Ivan all right," said Cal. "She was at my place. Look at this! I swear you'll say she didn't have this when she disappeared. Don't you see? She's been there. I wish she could talk." Cal shook the dog in excitement and frustration.

"I don't know what you're talking about. Put the poor dog down, she's hungry."

Cal put Frankie down and she ate greedily. He knelt beside her and fumbled at her collar. He held up a length of coloured cord that dangled there. "Look at this."

Reenie looked without interest. It was a cord made from several colours of thinner thread plaited elaborately together. She'd never seen it before, but it looked ordinary enough. "So? Ivan probably found it somewhere and put it on her before he, before he, um, ran away…"

Cal put his hands on her shoulders and shook her the way he'd shaken Frankie. "No. This is from where he's gone. I know it. It's mine. I made it, for granite's sake. I know. Ivan's gone to where I come from, and now he's stuck there and I'm stuck here. I thought so, but now I'm sure." He dropped his hands from Reenie's shoulders and suddenly punched at the wall with force, missing it deliberately at the last instant. "I could have gone back if only I'd been there at the right time. I should have worked it out properly. It's too hard."

"I don't understand. You're not making sense."

Cal ran out into the dark back yard. He stared at the sky. He turned around and around, hitting out at nothing with his fists, then slumped down, sitting on the cold ground.

"Stop it. You're crazy. What do you mean?"

"It's too hard. I can't explain."

"You said Ivan's stuck somewhere called 'there' and you're stuck here. What do you mean? And so what if Frankie comes home with a piece of cord from somewhere else? Why does that mean something?"

"It's not just a piece of cord. I know it. I made it. It's out of the top drawer in my room at home. You understand? My proper home where my mother and father and sister are. I used to like making stuff like that. Ivan must have been there, at my house. Maybe my parents and sister are looking after him. Frankie's been there, and now she's back here. If she got to the right place at the right time, Ivan must have worked it out too, and he missed out by a fraction, but the dog got through…and all this time I've been mucking about and missing chances…"

It was Cal's turn to hide his face in his hands. Reenie didn't know what to do. She patted him on the shoulder. "It's all right, Cal," she said.

"It's not all right. I've been stuck here for weeks. I was going home at long last when I ended up here. I wanted to go home after all that time." His voice shook.

"Where is your home?"

"That's the problem. It's right here in Willowvale."

"But you can't be from here. You only came a few weeks ago. I never saw you before in my life. Nobody did."

"I am from Willowvale."

"Well, prove it. If you're really from here, let's go now and find your family. Why didn't you go before and find them?"

"It's here but not here, and I can't get there."

"Here? Can't get there? Here is here. There is somewhere else. What do you mean? You're talking nonsense."

"I can't explain."

"Try." Reenie sat on the ground next to him. Uncertainly, she put her arm around his shoulder to comfort him.

"Nobody's done that since I left home," said Cal quietly.

"Do you have a girlfriend?" said Reenie, taking her arm away.

"No. And except for fighting, nobody's touched me at all since I left home—"

"Is that why you start so many fights?"

Cal looked at Reenie for a surprised moment. "I don't know. I get frustrated. I don't know."

"How long is it since you left home?"

"I was in O'Malley for a long time. Before that I wanted to leave Willowvale, I couldn't stand it…you wouldn't understand—but after a while in O'Malley I got tired of the place. It was so fake and they told so many lies about us, about Willowvale. So I came back. But somehow I ended up here, and it's the wrong Willowvale and I live in the other Willowvale and just when I'm finally sure how to get back, I miss the chance. There might not be drums again for weeks. I've been away for nearly a year."

Reenie was silent.

"And when you said Ivan disappeared from that spot, I thought he'd gone to my Willowvale, and now I know he's gone there, and it's probably my fault."

"What is your Willowvale?"

"It's like this one, but different. Some things are the same. Even some people…your dad, your grandfather, your grandmother… they're in my Willowvale…lots of people round town look sort of familiar."

"You're crazy."

Frankie finished licking her bowl clean and came across the grass. Cal stroked her ears.

"What do you mean, disappeared from that spot? Up near the power poles?"

Cal looked at Reenie. "You don't think I'm crazy, do you? It's important."

"No. Not really." She wasn't entirely sure, but she'd give him the benefit of the doubt this time.

"When I came back from O'Malley, I was at those poles. It was sunset. I went there because you can see our house from up there, or at least this kind of hut that my parents have a bit out of town. I thought I'd walk down there, sleep the night, then go home to our proper house in town. Now this is the weird part: I was looking down the valley. The sun was on the edge of the hills. Then the curfew drums started, like they always do at sunset..."

"Curfew drums? What are they?"

Cal didn't answer that question, but went on, "The drums started. I saw the sun go behind the hill. There was something wrong with the flying fox so I walked down to the valley...and when I got there, everything was different. I was here, not there. I haven't seen my family. Our house is still in this town, but someone else lives there, it's all different anyway...the whole town is different...no wall, no curfew, no...no...lots of things."

"Tell me about the drums. What's a curfew? You mean like, having to go home at sunset?"

"And I've been thinking and thinking so much my head aches. When I started down from the poles that day, the drums were still going. But now that I think about it, there were lights down there, and there aren't lights down there...in my Willowvale. I didn't think about it because I was so keen to go home. But now I think I'd swapped over then, right at the top of the ridge. I wait up there most days, but there aren't drums here very often. I wait...sometimes there are no drums, and sometimes they play, but too early or too late...it's too hard. Now I know for sure, really for certain that that's the way back. Frankie must have stumbled up there at the right moment and she's a dog, and she did it and I can't. And I saw Ivan up there a couple of days ago…I was angry with him—it's my own fault, not his—and then he disappeared…that must be when he went."

Reenie put her arm over Cal's shoulder again. He leaned against her as if to share her strength.

"Well, I'll help you," she said. "I hope someone on your side is helping Ivan, like you say."

"I know he's been to my house, met my family," said Cal.

A rectangle of light spilled out into the garden as the back door opened.

"Reenie? Where are you?" Mum called anxiously.

"You don't have anywhere to live, do you?" whispered Reenie. She felt Cal nod in the dark. His hair brushed her face. "You live in the bush?"

Cal didn't answer Reenie's last question. He stood up. "I'd better go."

"No. I'll ask Gran and Pop. They've got a spare room. Come on."

"I don't know. I don't want to be in the way—"

"Reenie? Is that you? What are you doing out there? Come inside."

"I'm here, Mum. Come on, Cal, we can sort it out. Gran loves looking after people. Trust me."

CHAPTER 9
OUTSIDE

Someone shook Ivan's arm and half asleep he thought it was John, back again. "Hey, stop that!"

"Shh. It's me." Cassie crouched on the floor beside Ivan's chair. Her eyes glittered in the candle light of the hall.

"Pip's knife. Where did you find it?"

"What? Let go of my arm. Why do people keep grabbing me?"

Cassie let go. Ivan put his hand into the pocket of the fur jacket to get the knife out. Nothing. He tried the other pocket, and his jeans pockets. Nothing but the woolly hat and scarf. His mind gradually woke.

"Oh, yeah. Your dad's got it."

"I have it now. I just want to know where you got it."

Ivan was silent for a moment. The musicians were playing a tune with a definite beat under a delicate melody. He saw the dancers swirl in one movement, turning and nodding. Mick was among them, dancing with the woman Ivan thought was Mrs Thompson from home, but here…well, she must be Dad's—Mick's wife. A young woman danced next to her, carrying a small child on her hip. That must be their daughter and grandchild. His half-sister and niece. Ivan looked away. Hadn't had enough time to get used to the idea of Dad having other people as family.

"I really miss him," said Cassie, her voice mournful.

"Who?" It took Ivan a moment to move his thoughts from Mick and that other family.

"Pip, of course."

"Who is Pip? People keep talking about him, but it's, like, a big mystery. Everything here is a mystery."

"I'll tell you, but not in here. Too noisy, too busy. Let's go outside." Cassie looked around. "Is anyone watching us?" Raven was playing one of his largest stringed instruments, his eyes closed and a blissful expression on his face. The music had clearly erased the incident with John from his mind. Thistle played a small mandolin-like instrument. Her eyes were sometimes on Ivan and Cassie, but the tune was intricate, and she frequently had to turn her attention to her hands.

"It's not that easy to sneak outside, but we can't talk here. What's Iris doing?" Cassie gestured toward the pleasant-faced woman at the door, who was chatting with a group of other women. "Maybe we can get out while Iris is on the door. She's nice," she said thoughtfully.

"What do you mean? Why can't we just go outside?"

"I know! Come with me." Cassie watched Thistle and Raven out of the corner of her eye for a moment then grabbed Ivan's hand. With Ivan in tow like a trailer Cassie moved toward the knot of people at the door. "Put your arm around my shoulders," she said, as they neared the door.

"What?"

"Just do it. Pretend you like me."

"I do like you—" Ivan stopped. "A bit..." He felt his face become hot, and no doubt red.

Cassie threw a quick glance at Ivan. "Just keep quiet," she whispered. "I'll talk. If I have to. Remember. You like me." She emphasised the word 'like'. Ivan stood, feeling his hands next to his body like the arms of a gorilla, heavy and ungainly. Cassie grunted, "Put your arm around me," but he couldn't make the gorilla arms move.

Cassie grabbed Ivan's hand, and with a neat dance-like movement twisted under it. Suddenly Ivan's arm rested across her shoulder. Cassie slid her closer arm around his waist and smiled at him. He couldn't help smiling back. He hadn't seen her smile before; like Thistle, her usual expression was serious. Maybe this wasn't so bad.

"That's better. Now come on," said Cassie. She steered him toward the door.

The conversation near the door continued between Iris and another eccentric-looking middle-aged woman. Cassie and Ivan were passing, nearly past, when Iris, without seeming to draw breath in the middle of her sentence, and without appearing to have seen Ivan and Cassie, said suddenly, "Where are you off to, young Cassinia?"

"Oh, hello, Iris. Just going outside for a breath of air. It's so hot inside."

"Yes, so it is, judging from the colour of your friend's face," said the woman next to Iris.

"A look at the stars, eh?" said Iris. "Don't catch cold."

Cassie smiled. "Yes, that's it. The stars." She steered Ivan through the door into the vestibule.

"Don't you stay out there long, Cassinia."

"You shouldn't let them," said another woman.

"It's so straight-laced in town. Let them go. You're only young once. They'll come to no harm," Ivan heard Iris say. She called after them in a louder tone, "Don't do anything I wouldn't do," and laughed. Her voice faded as the door shut behind them. Cassie and Ivan stumbled down the steps like inexpert competitors in a three-legged race.

"What was that about?"

Cassie kept her grip on Ivan's waist and pulled him into deep shadow in the darkness at the side of the building. He began to wonder why she had really brought him out here...no...His skin prickled. He felt her bony shoulders beneath his arm. She didn't have that wild jacket on for once. Her fingers dug into his side under his jacket. She turned her face toward him and suddenly Ivan remembered that Cassie was not only wild, but very pretty. Ivan felt his palms cold and his heart beat hard inside his chest.

"Show me where you found the knife."

"Why? I found it up where we met, at the power line—I mean the flying fox."

"I've been up there hundreds of time and I never found it…are you sure?"

Ivan could see Cassie's mind worrying at this fact like a terrier with a bone. But it was a pointless question. Surely he needed more questions answered than she did. "I told you where I found it. Tell me who Pip is. Your turn."

"Pip's my brother."

"You have a brother?" Oh. "So…where is he? He's not here?"

Cassie's voice wavered. "He is—was—is—older than me. He disappeared. A year ago." That made sense of the empty bedroom in Cassie's house, the bed piled with spare blankets, the model of the eagle hanging from the ceiling, John's remarks about the knife, and the fur jacket he was wearing right now.

Ivan felt Cassie's shoulder shiver slightly under his arm, realized that he still had it around her. "Don't cry." He hated people crying. "Do you want to see my house? It's not far. Just across the road and up a bit."

Cassie laughed shakily. "Okay. But I thought you wanted to know. About Pip. He was—is—the best brother ever."

"I do want to hear about him, but don't cry." Ivan put on a funny voice, like he did to cheer Anna up when she was sad. "It makes me go all weak."

"It's pitch dark," said Cassie.

"I know the way."

"Okay."

They made easy progress up the cement driveway that led from the hall to the road. Cassie wriggled out from under Ivan's arm, but she took his hand.

"Why aren't you allowed out of the hall? What did that lady mean about straight-laced? What did she think she was letting us get up to?" Ivan asked, as they felt the edge of the old roadside kerb with their feet. He felt his face redden again in the dark. *Oh yes.* He knew what she thought they were up to.

"In town everyone watches. There are so many things not allowed there. That's why we have the dances out here. No music allowed in town. No dancing. No anything that's not strictly practical. It's like a prison there. You can't do anything. Even Mum and Dad's garden is a bit dangerous. Not practical enough. The sundial and sculptures are too frivolous. I'm not meant to talk to boys; no girl is, not unless there's some good reason like schoolwork or a message from parents or something. Anyway, nobody wants to talk to me because our family is a bit odd. They don't trust us. We have the hut outside town, and they suspect we get up to something odd there, you know, the music. Iris hates all the rules and stuff, that's why she didn't mind letting us out. All the people at the dance are either ferals or townspeople who don't like rules. They know how to keep quiet." She shivered again. "We'd better not hang around out here. It's cold."

"Aren't you scared of the ferals? Isn't that why you carry on about safety? I thought they were dangerous." Cassie sneezed. Ivan realized that she only had on her party dress, fine for dancing, but not warm enough for outside on an August night. "Here," and he took off Pip's jacket and draped it over Cassie's shoulders.

"Thanks."

"Did your mum make it?"

"We make all our clothes, except stuff left over from before the disaster. Everyone does. That's why they were staring at you in town. You look like someone from outside, from O'Malley. That odd jacket of yours, and your strange shirt."

They stepped onto the cracked asphalt of the road, feeling their way with their feet. There was no moon. The starlight was not bright enough to light the ground, only to decorate the sky.

"So, why aren't you scared of the ferals? What about the wombat? You made enough fuss of danger last night when I first saw you. Hurry if you want to survive and all that." Ivan looked around, remembering the large wombat he'd glimpsed on the ridge, and the volatile moods of John. No matter what Cassie said about John being harmless, Ivan thought he was dangerous. He looked up. All he could see was the sky, peppered with stars, and the dark bulk of the ridge fringed with vague tree shapes.

"I—it's—I shouldn't tell you. You won't like it."

"What? Tell me what?" Ivan felt his breath catch in his throat for fear of what she might say.

"It's, well, it's like…"

"Yes?"

"You know how people tell fairy tales to keep kids in order? Bunyips, trolls, werewolves, that kind of thing?"

"Yes."

"Well, you know how I said that in town, they make you follow lots of rules and watch everyone all the time?"

Ivan nodded, then realized Cassie couldn't see him. "Yeah."

"Well, the animals and the ferals are just a kind of embroidered story to keep people in order. Most of the townspeople half believe it. Then there are the others, like us. Ferals are mostly just people who don't like town. The wombats…well, they're not too bad…you just have to keep away from their burrows. Surely you've heard of wombats?"

They reached the far side of the road. Ivan stopped to make

sure of his bearings. If they went straight ahead up the road opposite, and around the next corner, they would come to his house. His ex-house. But maybe Cassie didn't want to see it. It was dark, after all. 'See' was not an appropriate word.

"Maybe we should go back," said Ivan.

Cassie didn't answer.

"Cassie, do you want to go back to the dance? Tell me about Pip later."

Cassie's cold fingers gripped his hand. "Can you hear that?"

"What?"

"Motors. Oh no. Motorbikes, and they're coming to make trouble."

Ivan listened. Now that Cassie mentioned it, he could hear the sound of motorbikes droning. He guessed he hadn't noticed as soon as she did, because the sound of internal combustion engines was normal to him, though of course it was not to Cassie.

"Come on," said Cassie. "We'd better go back and warn them." She pulled at Ivan's hand and started through the darkness, back toward the square silhouette that was the school hall.

Ivan resisted. "I thought you said the dangers were just made up, fairy tales, that these things aren't really bad."

Cassie tugged at his hand. "Come on, come on. The outsiders really are dangerous. We have to get back to the hall."

The noise of motorbikes was close now. Ivan realized that most sounds were gentler here than at home, and now the engines' roar was fearful. Along the road, away from the town, the white glow of headlights appeared, unnaturally bright haloes shining into the air from below the crest of the road.

Cassie and Ivan hurried toward the hall. Ivan looked up the road and saw headlights appear, horribly bright, over the lip of the rise. Lots of them, a dozen bikes at least.

"Hurry, hurry," said Cassie. She started to run. Her foot caught in a pothole, she tripped and her hand wrenched at Ivan's so that they both fell. As Ivan hit the ground, all his small injuries came back yet again into his consciousness—the scraped ankle, pulled shoulder, the grazes from bumping into rocks, the scratches from falling into prickly bushes, and now a heavy thumping bruise on his hip.

Cassie gasped, "Ow! I'm all right," not sounding all right. "Ivan, this is important. If they see us they mustn't find out about the dance. Maybe if we keep quiet they won't notice the dance." She grabbed Ivan's hand again and tried to get up. "Don't tell. There aren't any lights showing. They might not notice. Don't tell."

Now the bikes were close enough to illuminate Cassie and Ivan with their headlights. Cassie struggled, tangled in her long dress. Trying to get up he lost his grip of Cassie's hand and couldn't find her at all. Engines filled his ears with noise and his nose with petrol fumes. Any other time today he would have been happy to hear and smell something so normal, but now he had a surreal feeling that he understood how rabbits felt in the lights of oncoming vehicles. He could see nothing but bright lights; couldn't locate Cassie in the confusion as bikes circled and stopped, engines still loud in idling.

"Don't, don't tell," Cassie hissed, her voice further from him than he expected. Motorbikes swirled around them, smelly and noisy. Ivan found himself outside the menacing circle, separated from her.

The motors hiccupped and purred. The riders laughed. It was not a happy sound.

"A girl." The speaker propped his bike and walked toward Cassie. "What a find. A pretty one, if I'm not mistaken. A village maiden in a party dress and a feral's coat. Just what we were looking for." Though the speaker's meaning was menacing, his voice sounded smooth and his actual words were strangely old fashioned. Before Ivan could move, the bike rider grabbed Cassie by the arm and lifted her onto the back of his bike. The rider shifted into gear, began to move off. Ivan saw the man who had spoken look over his shoulder at Cassie, whose fear was visible even through the panic that Ivan felt pulling around him like floodwaters. His stomach churned. This was no fairy story.

"Let's go," said the leader, revving his bike. The others revved their engines in reply.

What could he do? He couldn't let Cassie be kidnapped by these—these—pirates. Ivan didn't want to think about what they intended. He forced his feet to move and his mind not to consider the consequences. He dashed across the broken pavement, over the white-dazzling light and black-hole dark of the scene and, trying to think of nothing but action, leapt onto the pillion seat of the nearest motorbike. The rider was revving its engine, already lifting his foot from the ground to the footrest.

Ivan gripped the rear of the seat as the bike jerked forward. He felt the rider turn in surprise to try to look at him.

"What the flaming comet are you doing, you goanna-faced idiot?" shouted the rider, putting his foot on the ground again as the bike wobbled. "You're meant to be on Algernon's bike."

With something approaching relief, it dawned on Ivan that he was comparatively safe, at least for a few minutes, while this person thought he was one of them. The other bikes were ahead; his face was already in darkness. He could stay with Cassie, stop them from—from whatever...he made his voice as tough as he could. Thank goodness it had broken properly, or it would surely have squeaked like it used to. "Algernon got sick of me," he croaked gruffly.

The rider grunted. The other bikes were already fifty metres away. "Hang onto me properly then, you drongo," he said over the engine, "and bring your helmet next time." Ivan gingerly put his hands round the driver's stocky body as the bike accelerated up the road after the others. Cold air cut through his shirt as if it was nothing. He wished he still had Pip's jacket, or even the scratchy hat and scarf in its pocket. No, Cassie needed it more. Wind slapped his hair across his face and the bikes sped away from the school hall and from the town.

CHAPTER 10
MOTORBIKE GENTS

Ivan leaned closer to the leather-jacketed back of the rider for warmth, and to keep the buffeting wind from his face. The road was rough crumbling asphalt. Every bump through a pothole or swerve around a fallen branch made the sick feeling low in Ivan's stomach intensify. The motorbikes' headlights shone on patches of moving roadway. Ivan tried to work out where they were going. This was the road leading out of town beyond the school. He was aware of the tall pines that guarded the cemetery leaning darkly toward the road— then gone. Now Ivan could tell they were in more open space; the place that in his world Dad called 'ten-acre land', big houses each in the middle of a paddock with its own dam, avenue of spindly saplings and perhaps a horse or a couple of sheep to stare at passing cars. There were no lights, so Ivan guessed it was all different now.

Following the other bikes, Ivan's rider swooped around a bend onto a dirt road. Ivan was surprised to see lights here. They shone from the windows of a large two-storey house that seemed more like something from his world than this. The bike suddenly jolted so that Ivan couldn't even try to recognize the house; all his attention was on not falling. His curiosity had to be saved for later.

The bike turned again, and on the skyline were the skeletons of some industrial buildings that in Ivan's world presented the unprepossessing 'Gateway to Willowvale'.

So we're on the main highway now, Ivan thought. It was too dark to see anything much except the splash of light the headlights threw to the ground, the red eyes of taillights and the slight difference in colour between the sky and hills. If there were any stars, Ivan was too cold to look at them. He huddled behind the rider's broad back and concentrated on staying as warm as he could. How long did it take to get hypothermia? What about frostbite? How about falling unconscious from the bike and landing dead on the dusty verge like road kill? He hooked his fingers through some straps on the rider's jacket.

After some time the bike stopped with a jerk of brakes. Ivan's hands grasped and he managed to keep his balance more by reflex than skill. One by one around him the riders cut their engines. During this small interval Ivan held tightly to the back of the rider's jacket, mentally shaking himself. It wasn't a dream. He was too cold.

There was a shout from one of the bikers and noise and movement crashed through the momentary silence. A figure ran flashing in and out of the disjointed lights, in and out of visibility. A bike toppled and fell on its side with a thump. Ivan's rider dismounted, but Ivan's cramped fingers still clutched at his jacket. They fell off the bike together. There were more shouts and Ivan heard Cassie's voice among them.

"Grab her, Arthur!" someone yelled. Ivan struggled to get up but his feet were numb with cold and he fell again as the rider got up and steadied his bike.

Cassie yelled, "Let me go!"

"Stop!" said Ivan, but no-one replied. The rider shoved him aside with his boot and moved his bike so that the lights pointed toward the sounds of struggle. The other riders did the same, and in the centre of the ring of bikes Ivan saw Cassie and a man who was twice her size, the man who'd thrown her onto the motorbike outside the hall. Ivan's heart raced faster than fast. He had to help her. He got to his feet and stumbled numbly into the ring.

"Wilfred, you blind wombat, get back here," yelled his driver.

"Shut your cake-hole, Sinclair," came a voice from across the ring of lights.

That was probably the real Wilfred. Now was his only chance to act. He crossed the few metres to the centre of the circle and grabbed the man's arm.

"I'm over here, Sinclair, you spangled drongo," someone said.

"Arthur, what do you think you're doing?" yelled another voice.

Arthur's arm had more muscle in it than the whole of Ivan's body. He shook Ivan off with a casual angry gesture, as insignificant as swiping away a fly. But small as the effort Arthur used to rid his arm of Ivan, the distraction took his attention from Cassie for a second. As Ivan reeled back he saw Cassie writhe in Arthur's grip, twist and kick. Arthur lost his hold on her and she landed on her feet, yelling.

"Where's Pip? Pip! Are you here?"

Ivan tangled with a tussock of grass in the shadows. Everyone had forgotten him. The riders stood, lit by the crossing headlight beams. Arms folded high on their chests, hands in belt loops, feet apart. Ivan saw no sign of recognition on their faces.

"Pip, Pip, the toughest boy in Willowvale," shrieked Cassie desperately.

A snort of laughter went round the ring.

"No-one in Willowvale is tough, tweety-pie," someone said, and the ring took a step forward.

Cassie took an involuntary step back, though there was no 'back' in the centre of the ring. Arthur was amused. "No Pips here, pipsqueak," he said.

"Come on, Arthur, stop mucking around," someone said.

Arthur paid no attention to this but bent over close to Cassie. "No Pip. No excuses. No messing about."

"You know him!" screamed Cassie so suddenly and piercingly

that Arthur recoiled. "My brother. You must know him. He's with your—your tribe—give him back." Her voice cut through the frost-glittered dust that churned around the boots of the riders into the light, and rose, a mixture of anger and sadness like the cry of a bird in the night. Ivan realised Cassie had long been saving this rage and despair in her heart, and now it came out as her only means of defence and as a distant hope, to be brought to light only at the one right moment, to be used once and once only. *She hasn't seen me since Arthur threw her onto the bike, she must think she is alone*, thought Ivan with a swooping feeling of pity for her.

Arthur hesitated—he appeared surprised.

"This is his coat—he left with it, but it came back—you must know it—it's the only thing he took that I've seen for a year—he ran away with you and I want him back. I've got his knife, too..." Cassie's anger flagged.

No, thought Ivan. He tried to send her strength—the anger was protecting her—he hoped he was still forgotten—he shivered as his body remembered that he was dressed in only a shirt and jeans in the ice-ridden winter midnight—shivered with fear as he saw the ring of uplit faces.

Cassie roused herself again. She flung her arm upward in an arc, knocking Arthur's approaching hand aside. "My brother Pip. You have to know him. Don't touch me."

Arthur's voice was louder than Cassie's, and rougher. "Shut your cakehole, girl."

Cassie shook her bony fist defiantly in his face.

"Be still, mosquito," said Arthur. He took her by the elbow.

Ivan readied himself to intervene, pointless suicidal gesture as it would be. Cassie looked as if she'd punch Arthur in the teeth, if only she were able.

"Show me this feral coat." He spun her round. "Nice work in it. Feral coats sell for a good few dollars in the high street shops. I'll do a deal with you, girl."

"No. It's my brother's. It's all he left but his knife—I'm not afraid to use that, you know."

"You're in no position to bargain, or threaten for that matter, squeak."

Cassie tensed. If she had been one of the cats whose pelts made the coat, her fur would have stood on end. "Just think," she said quietly.

"Say 'please'," growled Arthur. The others stirred restlessly. Ivan shrank into the shadows, ready to—to do what?

"Please?"

"Pip's a stupid name. No Pips here, squawker."

"Okay, then." Cassie appeared to have an idea. "That's a nickname. I'll tell you his real name, his true name. Callitris. Callitris. You must know him. He's sixteen, no, seventeen years old by now. Skinny. Red hair."

The bikies laughed loudly and took another step closer.

I have to do something. She hasn't got a hope of getting out of this. Ivan crouched in the shadows, ready to act. He had no idea how. He watched Arthur laugh, but didn't hear for the pounding of blood in his ears. He didn't hear anyone approach him from behind. The hand that grabbed a fistful of his hair and pulled him farther into the shadows made him start to shout, but straight away another hand went over his mouth, catching the sound.

"Get up," hissed a voice, forcing Ivan upward by pulling his hair so that he was forced to rise. "And keep quiet. Or else."

Ivan considered biting but the hand was covered with a dirty leather glove.

"Keep quiet or I'll—I'll..." It was a young voice, a boy's voice, a boy about his own age. He shook Ivan by the hair to emphasise his point.

Ivan grunted in pain. The hands gripped tighter. The boy pushed him away from the circle of bikes.

"No!" Ivan tried to shout.

"Quiet." The boy shoved Ivan behind a large tree.

"Who are you?" He took his hand off Ivan's mouth.

"I'm Wilfred."

The boy hit Ivan in the stomach. "You are not. I'm Wilfred. So, who are you?"

Ivan gasped for air. His mind raced. *Don't let him know who I am,* he thought. "I'm new. They thought I was you."

The boy punched him again, but in a thoughtful way, not hard. "So? Your name?"

Ivan didn't want to tell his name. All the bike riders seemed to have old-fashioned names. "Bill," he said. "Now let me go."

Wilfred's voice sounded suspicious, but his aggressive manner dropped away. "I don't remember you."

Ivan edged away around the tree trunk. He could hear Cassie's and Arthur's voices. He had to get back—but first—an idea—perhaps Wilfred could help him, even if he didn't want to. He'd know things. "Do you know this person the girl is talking about?"

"Nup."

"Pip. It's an unusual name, you'd remember."

"I don't know any Pips. Except in oranges."

"Callitris, then. You wouldn't forget a name like that. Or," Ivan had an idea, "maybe he had some other name."

"Why are you asking?" Suspicion crept back into Wilfred's voice.

"Well, he might actually be one of...us. You know." Ivan made a wild guess. "Our, um, code, doesn't look, um, kindly on um, stuff like that, you know, with one of our sisters, if you know, um, what I mean."

Yes, he'd hit the jackpot. He heard the other boy rustle uneasily as he moved against the loose bark hanging on the lower part of the tree.

"You mean the Gentlemen's Honour. Oh, festering wombat droppings, yeah."

Think quickly, you idiot, Ivan silently urged him. "What was that other name she said? He might have chucked the name Pip, or Callitris, you know, they're not your, I mean our kind of names, he'd have guessed that soon enough," whispered Ivan, hoping that he could somehow jolt Wilfred into saying something useful. "Cal-something, Calvin, Calmont? Cal—Cal, cal, cal. Do you know a Cal, Wilfred?"

"Nup."

"Think."

"Why? What's in it for you?"

Oh no. Keep Wilfred on side. "The Gentlemen's Honour. You know, it would be really bad if she's someone's sister and we, um accidentally did, um the wrong thing. And…she does remind me of someone. A lot. You don't see, um, that curly reddish hair often…"

Ivan tried to crane his neck around the tree to see what was going on. Cassie wasn't visible, but he heard Arthur talking. That was a good sign. Ivan turned the contents of his brain over like a person searching for lost keys. Cassie is so sure Pip was with these people, that he knew them. But his name meant nothing to Wilfred. Wilfred didn't know either name, Pip or Callitris. Could he have another nickname? What did Callitris mean? It rang a vague bell in Ivan's mind, but he couldn't get hold of the knowledge. Ivan groaned out loud in the effort to think. "Oh, yes!" he grabbed the thought before it could get away. Thistle is a plant, and Cassie is really short for Cassinia, wasn't that a plant too? What was Callitris? Raven was a bird—no, Callitris isn't a bird…yes, a tree! "Wilfred! Know anyone with a tree name? A bit older than us? Come on, Wilfred, think. It's important."

"You're as dizzy as a tree full of drunk koalas. Oh, there's Gummy Gladstone. But he's old. Rides a three-wheel bike on

Sundays. There's Rowan. But he has black hair—"

"Come on, think. A tree. Someone called after a tree." Ivan heard Cassie speak. Her voice was rising to a panicked pitch again. "No ideas?" What kind of tree was it? That would help. Not gum trees. Pine? Thistle and Raven knew native plants, he was sure...native—"Native pine?"

No recognition from Wilfred. Cassie's voice grew higher and louder, like a wild bird trapped in a cage. Arthur interrupted gruffly.

Birds. Those crazy birds that eat the seeds in the native pines— Pip—seeds..."Hey, Wilfred, was his name Gang-Gang? Galah?"

Wilfred said nothing. Ivan guessed he shook his head in the darkness, trying to hear what Arthur was saying.

What else? Gang-gangs have bright red crests. "Didn't the girl say he had red hair? Are you sure it wasn't Gang-gang?" he persisted. "Red hair. There's something important about red hair."

Wilfred moved his feet in the fallen bark. "Yeah, I remember now, there was a bloke, red hair, you're right, a young guy, a bit older than me. He left just about the time I came. Not Gang-gang, that's not a name, that would be silly—"

"Well, what was his name? Come on, Wilfred, think. It's important. You know, the honour of the, um, group," urged Ivan, feeling that there was something he should remember, himself, as well.

"Radcliffe!" said Wilfred suddenly. "It was Radcliffe. I remember him. He had red hair. Always spinning a yarn that he came from—oh, from Willow Village or some six-finger place like that—" before he finished the sentence, Ivan was out from behind the tree and halfway across the circle of motorcycles. He had to take the chance that this name was the right one, and that the name would protect Cassie from the harm these people could do to her.

CHAPTER 11
BIG POTHOLE

Back on the pillion seat, Ivan could hardly believe the turn of events of the last hour. His wild guess at Cassie's brother's alias had produced a transformation so surprising that he still had to shake his head inside the spare motorcycle helmet, and shrug his shoulders, sheltered from the wind by an old leather jacket someone had produced out of a pannier, to make himself believe that what had happened was real.

"You're Radcliffe's sister?" Arthur had said in tones that travelled from horrified through uncertain and embarrassed to friendly in the five syllables.

"Yes, she is!" yelled Ivan in case Cassie said the wrong thing in confusion. Maybe she knew nothing of the name Radcliffe.

Arthur beckoned Cassie into better light. She approached warily. Ivan moved closer to the centre of the ring, followed by Wilfred. "Let's have a look at you," said Arthur. "Well, I believe it's true. No-one but his sister could have that hair, that face…that…that boldness…"

Ivan stared at Cassie too. Was there something slightly familiar about her, like a misty thought he couldn't quite catch in a corner of his mind?

Suddenly the bike riders were all cordiality. Someone lit a campfire and an oddly domestic picnic appeared—tea from flasks, fruit cakes, sandwiches.

"So where's Pip, I mean Radcliffe? I can't wait to see him."

"Good old Radcliffe, it was like he'd been born on a bike," someone said in reminiscent tones.

"Yes, a natural he was; young, though. Fast learner…"

"So he's not here?" persisted Cassie. "Why? Where is he?"

"You haven't seen him?" Arthur seemed surprised. "He left weeks ago. Haven't seen him since. Changeable young fellow."

"But he hasn't come back," said Cassie. "Where can he be?"

There was a cough from Wilfred. "He had a job in O'Malley. He was saving up for his own bike, wasn't he?" Wilfred looked uncomfortable as everyone's eyes turned to him. "He, um, might have gone back to O'Malley to get the bike, if he hasn't gone to Willow Village, um, vale."

There were murmurs of agreement around the campfire, and everyone buried their faces in cups of tea and slices of cake. Cassie sighed and said, "Well, then, can we come to O'Malley with you? I really want to find him."

Ivan's heart sank. *How am I going to get back to Willowvale and get home if I'm in O'Malley?* He opened his mouth to say this to Cassie, but she was talking intently with Arthur, and he couldn't get a word in. Soon the picnic was finished, the flasks packed away. Ivan didn't know when he'd get back to Willowvale and to the ridge to listen for those sunset drums.

Now Ivan pulled his hands into the too-long sleeves of the borrowed jacked, hunched himself inside it, and concentrated on staying warm. Mind over body. The road was sealed but riddled with potholes and the bikes swayed one way and the other to avoid them. Ivan had to cling attentively to the back of the rider, Sinclair, though he felt desperately tired and fought sleep unwillingly. The journey continued in a blur for about an hour, without much variety until the group of motorbikes stopped in a tight bunch in the middle of the road. Sinclair stopped his bike too. Ivan tried to guess where they were now, but past the headlights everything was simply shades of blackness. It was impossible to guess their location; surely they couldn't be far from O'Malley now, perhaps somewhere near Walagu.

The riders dismounted and walked up the road ahead, huddled down in their jackets, hands in pockets. Ivan climbed off Sinclair's bike and joined Cassie and Wilfred, who stood nearby.

"What are they doing?"

"Checking the road. It can change quickly, rock falls and things," said Wilfred.

Cassie said, "It's the crater. Come on, Ivan, you must know about the crater."

"What crater?"

"Everybody knows the crater—the meteorite—the lake—you know—meteor, kaboom, no more Walagu…" Cassie lost patience trying to explain to Ivan and turned to Wilfred. "This is great! I've never been here before! I wish it was light."

Ivan had no idea what she was talking about. "Is this a joke? If there's been an accident or something, this isn't funny. I'm going to see what's happening."

"Be careful, they're right near the edge," said Wilfred, but his warning was as incomprehensible as Cassie's explanation. Ivan strode toward the group of bikies. He was fed up with this weird world. It was confusing enough without people pulling his leg, deliberately making fun of him. Crater, huh. If he had to go on this fool's errand to O'Malley—and something in the back of his mind told him it was a fool's errand—maybe he should try to talk to Cassie about it again. No, she was in conversation with Wilfred now—if he had to go with them, then, why couldn't they move on? What was all this messing about? It must only be another thirty kilometres to O'Malley.

"Sinclair, what's up?"

Ivan was surprised to find that the bike riders were standing in a single row across the road. He turned to look for Sinclair, but their faces were in shadow. Ivan took a step backwards to get a better look at them and felt the edge of a pothole under his heel.

"Stop, you fool!" Someone jumped toward Ivan and grabbed for his hand as his foot slipped into the pothole. There was an odd clattering from the road ahead and an angry shout from below. "Can you chough-brains stop dropping rocks? You nearly killed us."

Ivan's foot slipped again on the lip of the pothole as this mystifying shout reached his ears. It sounded as though Arthur was below, but how could he be? Both Ivan's feet slipped out from under his legs. A hand that had grabbed at him missed its grip. He saw the row of helmeted heads flash silhouetted across the starry sky for a split second, then he was sliding down a steep bank, yelling in fright. There were yells from above and below, too. Small stones rolled with Ivan in the dark, making a musical clattering sound that disappeared as if into a large space. With a thud, Ivan landed on a flat surface, winded. He had the presence of mind to curl up as a shower of pebbles and small rocks hit his helmet, then lay still wondering if he'd broken any bones. As the last of the falling stones bounced to silence, Ivan heard voices both near and above. The beam of a torch shone on his face and he uncurled.

Arthur redirected the torch beam from Ivan's dazzled eyes and said, "Are you hurt, lad?"

Not knowing the answer to this question, and still struggling to refill his lungs, Ivan sat up, gasped in a chest full of air, and felt himself for blood. Not much. Only about a couple of dozen bruises and grazes. His voice returned. "What happened?"

"You damn near fell all the way," said Arthur gruffly. "He's alive," he shouted upwards in response to the calls that bounced down like echoes of falling stones. "Can you stand?"

Ivan could stand up, shakily.

"Look here." Arthur directed the beam of his torch up to the place where a line of worried faces flashed white, and down past the far edge of the ledge on which the riders stood. Ivan saw the beam disappear into nothingness. There was a huge, crumbly hole here that had never existed before. His stomach lurched. "Lucien, the boy didn't know about the crater. They breed them ignorant in Willowvale, don't they?"

"The road's dangerous here. We're checking it before we go on," said Lucien politely.

Ivan couldn't answer. He was shaking all over.

"Sit down. We'll take a look round the next bend or so and come back for you in a few minutes."

With trembling legs, Ivan lowered himself to sit leaning against the bank. He waited, shivering with shock and many small hurts for Arthur and Lucien to return.

There were voices and a torch's small moon showed from the other direction. Cassie ran to Ivan. "Are you all right?"

Wilfred shone his torch over the edge as Arthur had done, and returned without comment.

"Can you walk? Are you hurt?"

"I'm okay. This is the biggest pothole I've ever seen in this road," Ivan joked feebly.

"So you've really never heard of the crater before?"

"I don't understand. No, of course I haven't."

"You haven't heard of the meteorite?"

"No."

"The famous meteorite that hit us twenty-five years ago and destroyed Walagu and everyone for miles around, that diverted the river into a huge new lake and cut off Willowvale? I thought everyone in the world would know about it."

Ivan didn't feel like trying to take in this information. He understood the existence of the crater now. He didn't want more details. He stood up, wavered.

Cassie caught hold of him. "Are you sure you're okay?"

"Yeah." Ivan did appreciate Cassie holding his arm, even if he was okay. "Let's go back up there."

"I'll wait for Arthur and Lucien,' said Wilfred.

Cassie and Ivan limped up the way Cassie had come, which was a steep gravel road that looped in one hairpin bend to the point where the old ground level resumed and the others waited. There were cries of "He's all right," and Ivan was thumped painfully on his bruised back in congratulation for surviving, then there was a shout of "All clear," from below and soon Arthur, Wilfred and Lucien reappeared.

The road down the side of the crater was winding and steep, and surfaced with loose, slippery gravel. Ivan felt no urge to fall asleep now. His bruises and grazes throbbed in time with the engine and with each bump over a rut or stone. After what felt like an interminable series of hairpin bends and steep descents, the road became level, though it still wound around buttresses of shifty stones piled precariously to the top, seen flashing past as the headlights flicked over each one. Ivan realized that the road skirted the edge of the lake. He felt moisture in the air and saw the glitter of water reflecting the lights of the bikes. The noise of motors echoed from the steep sides of the crater and away across the water.

Ivan wondered what the next surprise would be in this journey. Clearly nothing was going to be predictable. The taillights of the bikes strung ahead like a ruby necklace. Now he thought he saw unlit buildings ahead, and lights high on a hill. The bikes slowed to negotiate a barrier that marked a change in the road from rough stones to smooth bitumen. Ivan saw an odd, modern building by the water. "What's that?" he called out to Sinclair against the noise of the engine.

"It's the yacht club. The resort's up the top."

"Yacht club? Resort?"

"They've been here for years. There's a ferry tour and water sports, a hotel, restaurants, and the longest waterslide in the southern hemisphere," said Sinclair over his shoulder.

Ivan thought he had misheard among the engine noise. "You sound like a tourist brochure."

"I'm the manager of the hotel. It's my night off."

Ivan had no response to this.

The shut up boatsheds and waterside cafés looked like sculptures in the headlights. They passed holiday apartments and Ivan realized with a slight shock that their entrances were lit with electric lights. The stark broken rock of the landscape was not softened by vegetation except for potted palm trees existing in a pathetic attempt to make the place look tropical.

The road bent sharply and began to ascend the side of the crater. It was easy compared to the descent—now the road was smooth, sealed bitumen. The hotel and restaurant complex at the rim of the crater was brightly lit with neon lights. Loud music pulsed out into the road and Ivan saw people in party clothes dancing as the bikes passed a glassed-in terrace. Then they were on the highway as Ivan remembered it—white lane markings, reflective signs, speed limits. Sinclair said something over his shoulder that might have been, "nearly there." Ivan started to wonder if the O'Malley they approached was the one he knew.

CHAPTER 12
IVAN AND CASSIE IN O'MALLEY

It was difficult for Ivan to get a coherent impression of this O'Malley. They passed through wide boulevards and roundabouts that looked the same as ever. But when the bikers stopped to say goodbye before heading their various ways, they assembled in the car park of a take-away restaurant that Ivan found very odd, coated in pink cement with a curious structure on the roof that he couldn't see properly. It might have been a giant sculpture of a kangaroo made of many-coloured aluminium bars. His brain couldn't process it, so he ignored it.

The group stood in a ring. "Well, here we are in O'Malley. What do you want to do?"

"Look for Pip—Radcliffe," was Cassie's prompt reply.

"It's midnight. Not now."

"They can stay with me. My mum won't mind," said Wilfred.

The others sounded relieved. "Righto, we'll drop you off."

Wilfred's house was in a well-lit street of identical houses, all neat and built of concrete in pastel colours, like a row of iced cakes glowing under amber street lights. Wilfred's mother, as predicted by Wilfred, was happy to have two strange teenagers arrive on her doorstep in the middle of the night. She reminded Ivan of Anna's Barbie doll. She made up a bed for Cassie in a spare room while Wilfred set up a mattress and blankets for Ivan in his own room.

In the kitchen, sizing Ivan and Cassie up with an experienced motherly eye, Wilfred's mother said, "Call me Berenice, dears. You look worn out and half starved. While Wilfred finds you some pyjamas—Wilfred—" Wilfred disappeared into the corridor again, "—I'll make you a hot drink." Ivan's mother was nothing like a TV advertisement mother; sometimes he'd wished she was. Berenice was disturbingly like one. He took back the wish.

Cassie's face, while Berenice made the drink, gave Ivan a picture of himself when he first arrived at her version of Willowvale. Berenice opened a green-enamelled fridge, which glowed from within and was filled with bright cartons. She poured milk into a shiny purple saucepan, added something Ivan guessed was strawberry syrup, and hooked the saucepan into a contraption of chrome and enamel. The liquid steamed and bubbled. Berenice unhooked the pan and poured the drink into coloured mugs. She took marshmallows from a jar and put them into the drinks, and sprayed pressurized cream from a can. Cassie and Ivan reached out for the mugs. "Wait!" Berenice reached for a shelf, picked up a container and shook chocolate powder over the concoctions.

The drink was hot, and very sweet. Ivan could tell from Cassie's expression that she had never tasted anything like it. She put hers down half finished. "Thank you Mrs um, Berenice." Ivan couldn't finish his, either.

"Where are you from, children?" Berenice asked as they put their mugs onto the bench.

"They're friends from school," said Wilfred quickly. "Their parents are at, um, at a party."

"Wilfr—" Ivan began, but stopped when he saw Wilfred's warning look. Cassie didn't seem to hear; she was staring with an awed face around the room, which was certainly very different from her own home.

Ivan knew with even more certainty that Cassie was suffering from culture shock when she emerged from the shower Berenice insisted upon, looking like a survivor from a perfumed flood, borrowed pyjamas soaked through, and looking like a very pretty drowned rat. "How do you make those things work?"

"Just turn on the taps," said Ivan unsympathetically.

"Oh dear, I'd better find you some more pyjamas," said Berenice.

"We don't have bathrooms like that," said Cassie.

Soon Ivan regretted his lack of sympathy. The plumbing in the bathroom was indeed complicated. It employed many taps, valves, and an unnecessary plethora of coloured lights and incomprehensible symbols on buttons, meant to be instructional—but not at all so. At least once he got it worked out, he was finally warm.

Actually, the house was too warm. In a few minutes, Ivan lay under a puffy feather quilt, sweating into Wilfred's spare pyjamas. While Wilfred was taking his turn in the shower, however, despite the heat, Ivan fell asleep.

Ivan woke with a sinking feeling. Did he have a maths test at school today? Was that big history assignment due? He opened his eyes and saw the blue-painted walls of Wilfred's room and sunlight coming through lace curtains of a geometric design. Wilfred was a lump under his bedclothes. The smell of waffles came from the kitchen. Relieved that neither the maths test nor the history assignment were to be faced this morning, Ivan got up and looked around for his clothes. He had no idea where he'd put them. They weren't on the floor near the bed. *Maybe in the bathroom.* Ivan threw on the biker jacket, which was beside his bed, and went to look. In daylight the bathroom was even more astonishing, filled with the strange plumbing and decorated in overpowering pink and blue with an even more overpowering scented air freshener. He must have been too tired to notice last night. Ivan retreated. There was nothing to do but go to the kitchen. The smell of waffles was enticing.

A couple of hours later, full of waffles and pineapple juice, Cassie, Ivan and Wilfred got up from the breakfast bar.

"It's a shame you all insist on wearing those disreputable-looking jackets. Wilfred, you're not planning to wear that disgusting leather one you try to hide from me, are you?"

"I am going to wear it. Today's Friday. I don't have to go to school. You should know that."

"You can't expect me to remember all your movements," said Berenice. "School or not, I insist you go out looking decent."

"Oh, all right," said Wilfred, and disappeared into his room.

"Would you like to borrow one of my coats, dear?" said Wilfred's mother to Cassie.

"No thank you, Mrs, um, Berenice," said Cassie. Ivan was not surprised that she refused to be separated from Pip's jacket.

"I could lend you a nicer jacket, if you like. It might be a bit big, but you wouldn't look such a fright," said Berenice.

Cassie pulled Pip's jacket around her and looked as if she was considering leaving the house immediately, dressed in satin pyjamas.

"Don't take offence, dear, none was meant." Berenice bustled around, pulling clothes out of an appliance that Ivan thought was a clothes dryer. "Anyway, I couldn't put that evening dress through the washing machine or dryer, dear, it would have been ruined," she said. "You'll have to borrow something to wear under that jacket." Soon Cassie was rather unwillingly fitted out in a pair of pastel yellow jeans belonging to Berenice, held up with a large silver belt, and a frilly pale green shirt. As she insisted on wearing Pip's jacket and her own large work boots, this failed to make her look particularly respectable in Berenice's eyes. Her encounter with plumbing the previous evening had left her hair looking wilder than before, though smelling strongly of frangipani shampoo.

"Where are you going, darling?" said Berenice to Wilfred as the three headed for the door.

"I'm taking Cassie and Ivan to town. We can catch the bus."

"I'll drop you into town." This was a command, not a request.

Through the long morning, Ivan waited for an opportunity to speak with Cassie. The thought continually went through his head that the only way back to his home was from the ridge in Willowvale. Yet Cassie's desperation to find her brother was equally important to her, he knew. The morning went on and on with no opportunity to speak to Cassie in private. Ivan decided to be philosophical about this, difficult as it was. There were things here he found himself enjoying, and he'd explode if he succumbed to the stress of not speaking to Cassie.

The O'Malley that they drove through in Berenice's pink car was more like the O'Malley Ivan knew than Cassie's Willowvale was like his Willowvale. It wasn't identical; despite the presence of cars and electricity, there were many differences. The insistent colours: the pinks, blues, peaches and yellows of Wilfred's house, which Ivan had assumed were purely Berenice's individual taste, were everywhere. Buildings were painted, people dressed in these colours. It became clear that the black leather jackets of the bike riders were a deliberate statement. Wilfred now wore a mother-approved outfit, clearly his regular clothes, in ice cream colours that matched the city. He bore absolutely no resemblance to the tough Wilfred of the night before.

As they crossed O'Malley, Ivan felt like a cake with three layers, probably all of pastel colours with too much icing. The first, uppermost part of him studied the city in fascination, taking in every detail. He enjoyed the feeling of unfamiliar familiarity now that he knew that most things would be unexpected and surprising, and some the same as usual. A second part of Ivan started to thoroughly enjoy being with Cassie and Wilfred. At home, Ivan had a couple of friends he'd known since primary school, but lately he'd begun to wonder if they all had anything in common any more. He knew he tended to hover at the margins of a social group, partly wishing to be included more, partly wishing to be alone. Now Wilfred, who in daylight was a slightly pudgy boy with smooth blonde hair and the accepting nature of a puppy—in fact he strongly reminded Ivan of a young Labrador—was friendly towards Ivan and Cassie in a natural way that took Ivan rather by surprise. The third part of Ivan, the part that wanted to get home, lurked close beneath the surface of the other two parts—waiting impatiently for the moment when he could speak to Cassie, start the difficult task of convincing her to return immediately to Willowvale. He had no idea how this task could be accomplished. There was something else, too, hovering on the edges of his mind, something that he couldn't pin down.

Berenice dropped the three off in the centre of the city, which looked much as it should. "Behave yourselves. Perso-text me if you need a lift home."

They waved goodbye and walked along a street lined with shops. In O'Malley Cassie looked wilder than ever, despite the pastel clothes. Now the jeans, shirt and belt served to make her hair, boots and jacket look completely crazy. Other girls were dressed smartly in the ubiquitous pastel colours, their hair cut and straightened. There were stares and surreptitious giggles as they walked along.

After walking a couple of blocks along a shopping street, Wilfred turned into a side street and continued for several blocks. The shiny clothes shops and cafés disappeared. This street was dominated by mechanics' workshops and car-part suppliers. Ahead was a business that displayed its purpose with a motorbike mounted on a tall black pole. Wilfred led the way into the workshop.

"I'm saving up for my own bike, they sell reconditioned ones here. I think this is where Radcliffe was getting his from. I'm pretty sure it is. We might find out something…"

"Where did he work? We can go there too."

"In town. We'll go there after."

"Weren't we going to meet the guys—weren't they going to help us too?"

"Yes, but, um, later. I'm waiting for them to contact me."

The three stood in the cavern-like shed that housed the workshop, uncertain of what to do next. At last one of the mechanics looked up from his work and saw them.

"Hey! What are you kids doing in here?"

Wilfred looked down at his clothes. "I wish I hadn't worn what Mum told me," he grumbled. He pushed Ivan forward. "Don't talk too much, but go first. He'll talk to you. You look tough."

Ivan swelled with pleasure. It was the first time in his life anyone had described him as tough-looking.

"The bike gentlemen jacket," Wilfred explained.

"Oh yeah, of course."

Wilfred nudged Ivan forward.

"Hi. G'day."

The mechanic stood with arms crossed, spanner in hand. He didn't look friendly.. "We're not a crèche," he said. "Wha'd'ya want?"

Ivan cleared his throat. He felt anything but tough. "We're looking for a guy called Radcliffe."

The mechanic folded his arms more tightly. "Why? What's the little bastard done now?"

Cassie pushed forward. "He's my brother, you wombat turd."

"Cassie!" Wilfred came forward at last. "Sorry about that," he said to the mechanic. "Hello. Um, Radcliffe is her brother. She hasn't seen him for—"

"A year," Cassie filled the gap.

"She's worried about him. Um, remember me? I came in a while ago about a reconditioned bike. I'm a provisionary member, I was with Sinclair..." his voice trailed away into nervousness. The mechanic shifted his considerable weight and remained silent.

Wilfred cleared his throat. "I'm nearly a full member of the Gentlemen of the Road."

"The other puppy looks more like one of them. Girl looks more like one than you, for that matter."

"I'm only wearing these clothes because Mu—" began Wilfred, then quickly said, as the mechanic's eyebrows rose mockingly, "Look, all we want is to know whether he picked up his bike yet. The one he was buying off you."

"Picked it up weeks ago. Paid for it in cash. I haven't seen hide nor hair of him since."

Cassie looked as if she was about to ask more questions, but Wilfred took her by the arm and steered her toward the street. "Thanks, mister," he said.

Ivan nodded to the man, who started back toward his work. "Excuse me. Was he really such a bastard?"

"When he first came, he was. He improved with time. It was a nice bike I sold him, unusual one. All red it was; a lovely paint job, bought a red helmet too. Now bugger off. I'm busy."

Ivan took the chance of asking one more question. He could see Cassie and Wilfred out of the corner of his eye, drifting closer again. "Did he say anything about where he was going when he picked up the bike?"

"It was weeks ago. Hey, you're not the police, are you? You look too young, but—no." He laughed.

"I'm his sister, like I told you. I want to find him."

The mechanic properly saw Cassie for the first time. "You do look a bit like him. That wild look is difficult to hide, even in O'Malley." He put the spanner down and scratched his head. "There was one thing. He said he was sick of O'Malley and the bike was his chance to get out. Now clear off. I've got work to do."

CHAPTER 13
SUGAR

"So Pip's got a motorbike," Cassie said despondently, as they retraced their route to the shopping centre. "He could be anywhere. How on earth are we going to work out where he's gone?" Neither Wilfred nor Ivan had an answer to this. They continued in silence for a minute when Cassie said, "We've got to find out where he might have gone. Hey, Wilfred, weren't Arthur and those people going to help us?"

Wilfred didn't reply.

"Wilfred? Are we going to meet them somewhere?"

Wilfred's round fair face was red with embarrassment. "I—I don't know."

"They seemed keen enough last night," said Ivan.

"Yes, well, that's all very well, but…"

"But what?"

"I'm the newest member. Like a cadet, on trial. I'm not important to them."

"But they have that big 'Gentlemen' thing. Doesn't that mean anything?"

"I don't know. Look—I've got a few ideas. Let's go on with them."

"I don't understand," said Cassie.

Ivan understood. Wilfred was the youngest, newest, least important member of the Gentlemen. His trust in their reliability was probably based more on optimism than anything else.

Just then there was a roar of motorbike engines. Cassie spun around—Ivan knew that for an instant the sound took her back to the road outside the old school hall and to the panic, fear and confusion that brought them here.

Three bikes pulled up at the kerb. "That's Sinclair's bike," said Wilfred.

"Good day to you, young people," said Sinclair, removing his helmet.

Wilfred put his hands into his pockets and tried to look nonchalant. "Hello, Sinclair."

"Didn't you pups want to find out about Radcliffe?" asked Sinclair.

"Yes, we've been to Jake's bike shop already."

"I thought we could take you to talk to Aunty. She knows everyone. Hop on."

"Who's Aunty?"

"You'll find out."

Wilfred climbed onto the pillion seat of Sinclair's bike. Ivan and Cassie climbed onto the other two. There were spare helmets hanging on the saddles.

They passed through several suburbs, all like Wilfred's, all not entirely unlike the O'Malley Ivan knew. At last, after passing a small group of shops and through a series of streets that curved confusingly, they stopped in a street full of cement rendered houses painted in pastel tones.

"So tell us who this Aunty is? Will she help us?"

"She's a friend. Be polite. We'll see you in half an hour."

"You're not coming in?"

"Things to do, lad. Half an hour." Sinclair and the other riders, who hadn't spoken or taken off their helmets, waited while the three dismounted, then drove off with a roar of engines that echoed behind them along the quiet street.

Ivan, Cassie and Wilfred stood for a few seconds, somewhat surprised. "They did help you after all," said Ivan.

"Yes, I suppose so."

"Come on, come on," said Cassie. "We'd better talk to this Aunty, whoever she is." They looked around. They were standing on a grassy island in the middle of the turning circle at the end of a cul-de-sac, surrounded by a circle of houses. The houses were small, joined together and identical except for colour. "Can you remember which one Sinclair said?" Had Sinclair mentioned which house Aunty lived in?

Ivan and Wilfred shook their heads. They stared at the houses. "We'll have to knock on a few doors until we find her," said Ivan, heading for the nearest door.

Wilfred seized the back of Ivan's jacket. "No! That's rude. You can't do that."

"Why not?"

"You just can't. Nobody does things like that. It's not polite."

"Don't be stupid, Wilfred," said Cassie.

"It isn't done," said Wilfred. "Trust me. It won't help."

Cassie rolled her eyes toward the sky. "Well then, we'll have to work it out some other way."

"How?" Ivan turned on the spot. The identical houses whirled past his eyes in a blur of colour.

"Let's pretend we're, um, following an animal, looking for tracks. There must be something. Think. Who could this Aunty be? Brainstorm."

"A friend of the Gentlemen," said Wilfred.

"Someone who knows about Pip, I mean Radcliffe," said Ivan.

"You know, a person who is both those things must be a little...different from the other people here," said Cassie. "Let's look for something different." She started to walk around the footpath, looking intently at each house. Wilfred trailed behind her, gazing at the houses in a manner that indicated he had no idea what he was seeking. Ivan decided to stay where he was and get an overview. He rotated slowly again, letting his eye slide over each garden fence, letterbox, front façade. Minutes were passing. And if this Aunty was to tell them anything, if they were ever to find this still-elusive Pip or Radcliffe, they must work out which was Aunty's house. He felt dizzy. Despite their colours, the little houses appeared completely without individuality.

Even the gardens were similar. Ivan let his eyes go out of focus. His feet were still turning his body slowly around. Cassie and Wilfred approached the street that led out of the circle. Then Ivan saw something that was different. Not odd or strange, but in this relentless sameness and neatness a small piece of rough stone by a cement gate-post was a kind of variety.

Stumbling with dizziness, Ivan hurried across the roadway and reached the gate at the same time as the others did.

"Nothing, nothing and nothing," said Cassie." Sinclair will be back soon."

"Look!" Ivan pointed at the stone.

"A rock. So? There's nothing unusual about that."

"It's the only thing in the whole circle of houses that's at all different. This must be the house!"

Wilfred looked at the stone. "You're right. And you know what? I think it might be a souvenir from the crater—the meteor—it's a sign, a clue."

They opened the front gate and walked down a short path that led straight to the front door, only half a dozen steps from the street. Before they could ring the bell, the door opened.

The woman was about ten years younger than Gran, Ivan thought. She wore the pastel clothes that everyone in O'Malley wore. She had long iron-grey hair in a plait. When Ivan saw her hair, he realized that all the women he'd seen in O'Malley, and probably most of the men, too, had dyed hair of various shades. Without thinking he glanced at Wilfred's blonde hair. It looked real.

"I've been watching you. I wondered when you'd work it out," said the woman. "Come in. Hurry, hurry. I wanted to see if you lot had any brains." She shut the door behind them and said, "Down the hall, take a seat anywhere you like." She limped behind them, talking all the while. An electric kettle was bubbling on the bench that separated a sunny back sitting room from a small kitchen. There was the smell of melted cheese. "I thought you might like something to eat," she said, as she followed them into the room. "It's all ready." She put a tray of cheese scones and cups on a small table, then poured boiling water into a teapot and brought it to the table.

Cassie sat down on a fat floral armchair, took a bite from a cheese scone and fidgeted.

Aunty saw this and said, "Yes, I know Sinclair will be back soon. He tells me you want to know about young Radcliffe."

"Do you know where he is?"

"No, sweetie. I'm sorry, I can't tell you. I don't know where he is."

Cassie sunk down in her chair and put her hands over her face. Aunty put the teapot down and said, "Dear me, I forgot." She sat down next to Cassie and put her arm around her. "I never did manage a good hug with young Radcliffe, prickly boy, but one with his sister is just as good. You'll find him, honey, don't worry."

"Do you know anything that might help us find him?" said Ivan

"Yes, of course, I'm sorry. It's lonely for me here. I'm excited to have visitors. I lived in Walagu years, years ago before the disaster. I was staying with friends here when it happened. Oh, it was terrible. Walagu was gone. Everyone in Walagu was dead; my husband, children…I had no home, just like that…" Aunty took a sip of tea, which Ivan had poured while she spoke. "The authorities panicked.

Well, I don't think they had any idea what had really happened. They said it was some kind of attack—a bomb or a missile, or some kind of secret mine collapsing. I still wonder about that. It could have been. Nobody was allowed near the place where Walagu had been. That horrible hole was all that was left. It was bad enough here, I guess, with half the houses in the southern parts of the city flattened and all the trees knocked down facing away from the impact as if they'd been executed. People were killed and hurt here too. I thought perhaps I could go and live in Willowvale, but they said it was destroyed, and no-one was allowed past the crater anyway. There were guards and signs.

"But there's that resort there now," Ivan interrupted Aunty's torrent of words.

"Yes, later they decided it wasn't a missile after all and that it's not dangerous. Anything for a profit. I'm starting to wonder what it really was. Everyone pretends there never was a Walagu. All they're interested in is their fancy food and their yachts and their expensive hotels."

Aunty's voice trailed off and at last Cassie got a word in. "What's all this got to do with Pip, I mean Radcliffe?"

"Well, I'd made a new life here. Friends, job…it went on for years; things were okay, but I was restless and lonely. I found out about your Gentlemen friends." Aunty nodded at Wilfred. "I guessed they made little adventurous trips down past the crater. And then I found out about the black market in goods to Willowvale."

"Black market? What do you mean?" said Cassie.

"I found out that Willowvale was still there," Aunty said. "I decided to get a motorbike and find out for myself what it was like. Then I had the accident." She gestured at her leg.

"Accident?" said Wilfred.

"I came off my bike. Smashed my leg. When I got better I couldn't bring myself to try again. I had a head injury too, and couldn't go back to work. I didn't have the money for another bike. Anyway, a while back there was this young boy who'd been causing a bit of trouble for the Gentlemen. He'd appeared out of nowhere—"

"Pip!"

"Shh," said Ivan. He could see that Aunty's story was not going to be hurried, but would in fact be slowed considerably by interruption.

"—living under a bridge or somewhere. Pestering them to take him on as a provisional. He stole a bike and rode it round the city with them in full chase to prove he could do it."

"Pip," said Cassie.

"Jake at the bike shop was livid. It was his bike, you see. Radcliffe lived here for a while, not long. I found out he came from Willowvale; tried to get him to go home, or even send a letter with the black market traders, but he wouldn't. Eventually I packed up his fur jacket and sent it as a sign to his family—without telling him. I see you got it somehow. Radcliffe and the Gentlemen sorted themselves out eventually. Those Gentlemen are a changeable lot. I lost touch with them…they're old-fashioned about women, you know, want us to act like ladies. It got very boring."

"So can you tell me where Pip, Radcliffe, might have gone?"

"He came back to me one night. He was in a bad way. I thought he was drunk."

"No." Cassie put her cup down with a bump and tea splashed onto the table. Wilfred took a handkerchief out of his pocket and wiped it up.

Aunty went on as if Cassie hadn't spoken. Wilfred looked at his watch. Ivan ate another cheese scone, which was a pleasant contrast to the sugary breakfast at Wilfred's place. Aunty's sitting room was a contrast to Berenice's tidy pastel-bright rooms, too. The walls were covered with old photographs, framed newspaper articles and landscape paintings. On every flat surface were piles of books, mostly dog-eared and musty-smelling. An old-fashioned china cabinet with diamond panes in the door held not china tea cups but pieces of broken crockery, rocks, a dented silver goblet, empty picture frames, ancient children's toys, a rusty street sign and even a fragment of crumbled red brick.

"I think he'd been living with one of the younger Gentlemen," Aunty was saying. "He worked for Jake for a bit. But he had a talent for brushing people up the wrong way. I let him stay with me again—"

"When?"

"Not too long ago. He came in June. He seemed different then. He had a new job; he went to it every day. I thought he should have been at school, actually. But he faded. He was sad."

Cassie's face was very serious. "What are you saying, Aunty? You don't mean he planned to...hurt himself?"

"You are from Willowvale, aren't you?"

In the silence between Aunty's question and Cassie's answer, Ivan heard engines in the street.

"Yes."

"What's it like now?"

"It's a town. Normal. Not like here. Tell me about Pip. Radcliffe."

Aunty sighed. "He got quieter and quieter. He never went anywhere except to work. One day he didn't come back. I haven't heard from him since."

Cassie looked as if she was going to cry.

There was a knock on the door and Sinclair's voice said, "It's a long walk back to town."

Wilfred jumped up. "We have to go."

Aunty hugged Cassie again and gently pushed her toward the door. "I'm sorry. I have no idea where he went." She kissed Cassie. "Can you let yourselves out? My leg..."

Sinclair and the others dropped Ivan, Cassie and Wilfred off where they'd met, in the street near the mechanic's workshop. They walked to the city. Cassie walked with her face down, hidden in her hair. She shook Ivan's hand off her shoulder when he tried to comfort her.

Wilfred said, "Look, Cassie, don't give up, we can still find things out. I've got an idea. Follow me."

"All we know is that he had a new red motorbike, wanted to leave O'Malley, and was depressed. He could be dead," said Cassie dismally, over Wilfred.

They were in the shopping street, outside a shop front that was, if possible, more brightly decorated than the others. Wilfred went in. It was a café with a display of cakes and ice cream and a long menu of strangely named drinks.

Wilfred sat down at one of the small tables. Cassie and Ivan sat too. Cassie closed her eyes. "Why are we here? I'm not hungry."

"I think this is where Radcliffe worked."

Cassie's eyes opened. "Really?" She looked around. "That's hard to imagine." She closed her eyes again.

The service was not very good.

The waitress who eventually came to the table wore a uniform of red and white candy stripes. "Can I take your order?"

"Hello, Emily," said Wilfred. "She goes to my school," he said to Cassie and Ivan. "Three rainbow sundaes with added zing, please."

"I don't have any money," said Cassie. She looked at the waitress' uniform. "Do they pay you extra to wear that?"

"I can pay," said Wilfred hurriedly, "for the drinks, I mean."

Ivan felt in his pocket. Amazing. There was a five-dollar note there, well washed. He wondered if money was the same here, and how much a rainbow sundae with zing cost.

Cassie had shut her eyes once more. "This place is giving me a headache. I don't think Pip would have worked here."

Wilfred said to the waitress. "Hey, Emily, did a fellow called Radcliffe ever work here?"

"I don't know. I only started here last week. Remember, I used to work at Zapparelli's? I can ask around, if you like."

Ivan was looking around the café. On the wall there was a crowd of framed photos of people in striped uniforms in every imaginable eye-popping colour combination. *Employee of the month* proclaimed a sign above the photos. The total effect was painful. He could understand why Cassie, from the natural-coloured world of her Willowvale, couldn't cope with it. Ivan stared in a daze at the photos, idly admiring the effect the colours had on his eyes, reds and blues fighting for prominence, pinks and purples pushing at each other to partner with oranges and greens, black and white merely adding to the confusion.

With a jolt of recognition, Ivan realized that one of the faces staring out of the confusion of colours was a face he knew. His hands felt clammy. It was Phil. How could Phil's photo be here? Phil was back home on top of the ridge, yelling something incomprehensible at him the moment Ivan switched from his own world to this one. Phil the boy who made Ivan feel small no matter what he did or didn't do. Phil, who always managed to make Ivan look foolish in front of his friends; Phil who was the only person Ivan had been in a serious physical fight with...Phil who...who had a jacket almost exactly like the one Ivan was wearing now. Ivan groaned out loud and mentally kicked himself. Phil who had red wavy hair a bit like Cassie's wild orangey-blonde hair. Phil who had a pointed chin and unusual golden brown eyes and bony hands and an animal style of movement...like Cassie. Phil who, if he was Pip, had at least three different names...

"Cassie. Open your eyes."

"No. I can't stand it."

"I thought you'd like this place," said Wilfred, sounding disappointed. "A lot of my friends come here. I don't come so often, because I'm saving up for a bike. I think we can find out something about Radcliffe here."

"She does like it, Wilfred, she doesn't know it yet, that's all. Cassie. It's important." Ivan shook Cassie's shoulder.

"All right, all right." Cassie opened her eyes. "It's the combination of the colours and the smell that's getting to me."

It was true. The smells of vanilla, strawberry and other chemical reproductions of flavours were overpowering. Wilfred looked hurt. Ivan took Cassie's head in his hands and turned it toward the wall. "Keep your eyes open. Look over there."

Cassie looked at the wall of photos. "I've never seen anything so hideous. I'm sorry Wilfred, I'm sure I'll get used to it soon," she said, trying to turn back to the table.

"No, no no no *no*! Look! Look at the photos. The pictures."

Wilfred looked too. He smiled. "Yesyesyesyesyes!"

"Let her find it."

Cassie's eyes unwillingly scanned the wall of photos. Ivan held his breath. Cassie gasped. "That's him!" She leapt up and hugged Ivan, nearly knocking him off his chair, then ran to the wall, lifted the photo from its hook and brought it back to the table. "How did you know? Ivan? Are you psychic? Do we look that much alike?" She held the photo up next to her face so that Ivan and Wilfred could compare.

"That's him," said Wilfred. "He looks different in bike gear, though."

Ivan felt sick. He liked Cassie so much, despite her abruptness and intolerance of his ignorance: because of her bravery and independence, and he had to admit, her interesting beauty, as well as just because he liked her. Now she was Phil's sister. He couldn't put them together in his mind. And now he had to help her find Phil, who thought so little of Ivan that Ivan suspected Phil didn't even think of him as a person.

"Ivan. You haven't answered. How did you know that was him?" A plaque on the photo said *Phillip Smith, June.*

"I know him. He's in Willowvale."

"No he's not."

"I don't mean your Willowvale. My Willowvale."

"You know him? He's your friend?" Cassie was smiling.

"I know him." Ivan didn't know what to say. Cassie was so happy. He supposed that even horrible people might possibly be loved by their sisters, though it was hard to imagine anyone loving Phil. The thought made him think of his own sisters. Parents. Grandparents. All at home thinking he'd been kidnapped or run away or worse. His sisters. What he would give to see them now. Reenie who was only a year older than him, with her seriousness intenseness. Anna and her obsessions with something new every week, her unerring talent for leaving her things where he tripped on them. He wondered if Frankie had gone home when he lost her on the ridge. That would puzzle them. Would that help, or make things worse?

"Ivan?"

"Sorry. I was thinking about how I miss my sisters. It seems stupid, but I do. A lot."

"So you know Pip? Is he your friend?"

"He goes to my school. I know him…a bit. Look, we need to get back to Willowvale. He must have gone back there and somehow ended up in the wrong Willowvale. He's been at my school for quite a few weeks. And I need to get back there too. Don't forget my parents haven't seen me for—" Ivan counted the time he'd been away from home, "for two nights." It seemed like longer. So much had happened. "I need to get back there too."

Cassie suddenly became serious. "I didn't think of that. You can't imagine how bad it was when Pip…didn't come back. We must go back to Willowvale, go to your Willowvale, get Pip, take him home…take you home."

Emily arrived at the table carrying a tray with three glasses piled high with ice cream of various colours. She stared at the photo. "There was nobody here called Radcliffe. Oh. Is that the boy you were asking about?"

"Yes."

"But his name's…Philip," said Emily, reading the plaque. She put the drinks onto the table.

"Sorry if you don't like the sundae," said Wilfred. "I thought you would. It's my favourite."

Now Cassie thought everything in the café was wonderful. She propped the photo up against the sugar bowl that stood on the table, and shovelled her rainbow sundae into her mouth with sudden enjoyment. "He's got lots of names, my brother," she said to Emily.

CHAPTER 14
LEAVING O'MALLEY

At last Ivan and Cassie had the same objective. "Hurry up, Ivan, hurry up Wilfred—we have to go."

Ivan was glad to be ordered about by Cassie now. He quickly swallowed his sundae, which was as sweet as it looked. Wilfred ate his, but not as fast. "What's the hurry?"

"Two things," said Ivan. "One, we have to get back to Willowvale to get Cassie's brother. Two, I really need to go there as well. My parents will be out of their minds with worry."

"I don't understand. Why don't you just call them?"

"It's too complicated to explain," said Cassie, getting up from the table. "We have to go now."

"One more thing—" said Ivan.

"But Cassie," said Wilfred at the same time, "how are you planning to get there?"

"Is there any chance of getting a lift back with your motorbike gentlemen?" asked Ivan. Wilfred looked down into his glass. "I guess not. It's a shame you don't have your own bike yet," Ivan went on.

"He couldn't take two extra people anyway, even if he had a bike," Cassie pointed out. "We'll have to walk."

"Walk? It's over a hundred kilometres."

"If there's no other way, that's what we have to do."

Ivan wasn't very keen on this idea. "But what about water, food, night-time? It'll be freezing. It could take days and days. We need to plan."

Cassie sat down again. She held the photo of Pip in front of her as if searching his printed image for advice. Ivan turned over their resources in his mind. They had warm coats; he had no intention of giving back the old biker's jacket. They were young and fit, well, Cassie was fit, and Ivan had reasonable confidence in his strength...but there were, he guessed, three nights of sleeping outside on the ground; and likely four days of walking. Ice cream sank like a lead weight to the lower part of his stomach at the thought.

"It's still early. We can do it." Cassie said. "It will be an adventure."

Ivan thought wishfully of the regular bus service that connected O'Malley and Willowvale in his world.

Wilfred scraped the last of the ice cream from his glass and said, "I haven't got any ideas. I suppose we could try contacting Sinclair or Algernon or Arthur..." his voice didn't convey much hope of success.

There was an odd musical sound somewhere near. "What's that?" said Cassie. "Is that what your music sounds like? It's not very good."

Wilfred put his hand into his pocket and brought out a small device that Ivan guessed was the equivalent to a mobile phone. He pressed a button and a ribbon of paper rolled out of it. "It's a message from my mum."

Cassie looked surprised. "Can I read it?" Wilfred ripped the paper ribbon off the machine and passed it to her. "It's in code. I can't read it. What does it say? Amazing."

Wilfred took the strip of paper and translated fluently. "She's picking us up soon. I'll tell her where we are." He pushed buttons on the device and turned a tiny handle. The message went off with an electronic sound. "Mum will be here soon to take us home."

"But we have to go back to Willowvale," said Ivan and Cassie together.

"I know. But our place is in the southern suburbs. At least that saves a bit of walking. And even if I can't come all the way, I think I could give you some food and a couple of old blankets. That would be useful."

Ivan felt a little less nervous when he heard this idea, but not much.

"Do you think your mother would mind if I keep these clothes 'til I get home? I can't walk that far in my party dress. I'd wreck it, and it's not very warm. I could send the clothes back later with the traders."

"Oh, she'd probably let you keep them. She gets new clothes quite often."

"Really?" Cassie was as surprised at this as she had been at the message device. "I expect my trousers will last for years. Thistle's only had a few pairs ever since I can remember. She made her newest pair when I was nine."

"We'll wait outside," said Wilfred, not knowing how to respond to this remark. Ivan supposed that if he'd seen more of Willowvale than the school hall in the light of headlights, he'd understand. Wilfred went to the counter to pay for the sundaes. Cassie picked up the photo of Pip and put it under her arm.

"We should try contacting Arthur or Sinclair," Cassie said when they were outside on the footpath. She hopped restlessly from one foot to the other, waiting impatiently for Berenice to arrive. "They might help us. Do you have their, um, their message number in that thing?"

"Don't you have perso-texts in Willowvale?"

"We don't even have electrical telephone machines, but I know what they are. Do you have their numbers?"

"I don't think there's much point," said Ivan, but Wilfred took out the perso-text and handed it to Cassie.

"You try," he said.

Cassie took the device. She turned it over and around in her hand.

"I'll put in the number," said Wilfred, and did so. "Now you write the message."

"Do I have to know that writing code?"

"No, just put in the letters. See, press the button with each letter on it." Cassie entered letters, which spelled 'canyoutakeus-towillowvalecassieivan'. Wilfred took the device and fiddled with the rotating handle. The machine made a sub-musical sound. "It's gone," he said. "I don't expect they'll reply." He put the perso-text into his pocket.

They stood on the footpath, waiting for Bernice's pink car to appear, or for Arthur, Sinclair or Algernon to respond to the message. Time felt slow. Ivan thought the passers-by more and more artificial-looking the longer he waited, with their dyed hair and high heels, perfectly horrible clothes and stares at Ivan and Cassie. Cassie was oblivious to the stares, or returned them as blatantly as they were given.

A bunch of teenagers approached. "Hey. Wilf. How's it going?"

"Yeah, fine."

"Who are your friends?"

"Hello, I'm Cassie and this is Ivan." Cassie held her hand out, ready to shake hands.

The girl who'd spoken ignored Cassie's hand. She ran her eye up and down Cassie and then did the same to Ivan, as if she was a judge at a dog show. "Strange names. Strange kids. I'm surprised at you, Wilf."

"They look like Vaileys. Have you counted their fingers?" said a boy, and laughed.

"What would you know?" said Wilfred with a flash of the aggression Ivan had seen in the night. "Mind your own business. Leave my friends alone." He lunged toward the boy, who backed away.

"Actually, that Ivan one looks like one of those bikie guys, you know, a baby one," said another girl. "Aren't you always pretending to be one of them too?" She laughed.

"Wouldn't you like to know?" said Ivan.

"Let's see how tough you are, then," said the second boy, giving Ivan a shove on the chest. Ivan shoved him back, not too hard. The boy lurched backward more than the push justified and teetered on the kerb. Berenice's car approached. Someone caught the boy by the arm and pulled him onto the footpath, but there was no real danger. Berenice stopped the car by the kerb.

"Wilf's mum! Clear out, she'll tell my parents if she recognizes us," someone said, and the group vanished into the stream of people walking past.

"Strange friends," said Ivan.

"They're not my best friends," said Wilfred with emphasis

"I know some people like that," said Cassie. Ivan thought the same thing, but said nothing.

"Hop in, dears, we have to go," called Berenice from the driver's seat.

As they drove, Berenice said, "I want to go to see your Uncle Ben this afternoon, Wilfred. Can I drop Cassie and Ivan home?"

"I've got an Uncle Ben, too," said Ivan to nobody in particular.

"Thanks, that would be wonderful!" said Cassie.

"Where do you live?"

"Can we drop them off at the Crater Resort?" said Wilfred quickly. While Berenice absorbed this request, he said quietly to Ivan and Cassie, "That's as far as we can take this car, sorry."

"That's a funny place to live," remarked Berenice.

"Oh, we don't live there, we live—"

"—nearby," interrupted Wilfred.

"All right, sweetie. It's a bit out of the way, though." Berenice sighed as she stopped the car in her driveway and pulled the hand brake with marginally unnecessary force.

"Mum,"

"Yes, Wilfred?"

"You don't mind if Cassie borrows those clothes you lent her, do you? She'll send them back. She didn't bring anything, um, suitable."

Berenice paused with her hand on the front door knob. "I'll swap. That retro Vale-style party dress would fetch a fortune—" she passed a sharp glance at Cassie. "What do you say? You can keep the jeans and shirt."

"I…it's Ivan's Gran's dress. I can't…"

Ivan was surprised.

"She lent it to me."

"Take it or leave it, sugar. Of course, if you leave the dress with me, I won't feel I have to pass on any suspicions I might have about where you're from or what influence you might have had on my Wilfred."

"I can't. Where is the dress? Thank you for lending the clothes. I'll get changed again."

"Would you like to do a deal on your fur jacket then?" The tone of voice made this a demand, not a question.

Cassie hugged the jacket across her chest. "No way."

Berenice looked at her long pink fingernails. "Are you sure?"

"Mum, please." Wilfred went into the laundry and brought out the emerald dress on a hanger, brushed and dry.

"Well, tell me if you change your mind." Berenice's expression changed back to—almost—its usual empty sweetness. "I'll be leaving in a few minutes. Be ready."

Wilfred waited until Berenice went into her room to get ready, then hurried Ivan and Cassie to a hall cupboard. He took two blankets out, went to the kitchen where he found a box of matches and two shiny packets of a snack food Ivan didn't recognize, and two bottles which he filled with water. He snatched two large plastic shopping bags from under the bench and stuffed these items into them. "We'll meet you at the car," he called to Berenice. "Cassie, you'd better get changed if you want to. Keep those jeans on under your dress. Really. Mum won't notice. She's got dozens of them." Cassie went into the bathroom to change. Wilfred disappeared into his room and returned wearing his black leather jacket.

The drive to the resort took place in an awkward silence. Berenice abandoned the breezy pleasantness that had briefly reappeared a few minutes before. The presence of Wilfred's leather jacket and Cassie's evening dress and fur jacket were clearly irritants, but Ivan had a clear feeling that something else had changed Berenice's attitude to them.

The land on the way to the Crater Resort, once past the last of the O'Malley suburbs, was cultivated with varied winter crops and full of well-fed cattle and sheep. Cassie, not much noticing Berenice's mood, was fascinated. She had Pip's photo clutched on her lap. It was amazing that the café people hadn't stopped her from taking it; perhaps they hadn't noticed.

Ivan let his eyes slide indifferently over the passing scene, seeing more and more clearly in his mind's eye the difficult journey ahead and imagining his return home. He'd never walked a hundred kilometres before, particularly not in a place so isolated where everything hung from his own and Cassie's selves, their own strength of mind and body.

Vineyards and fields of broccoli slipped rapidly past. The buildings of the resort came into sight. Berenice stopped in a car park that had a fine view of the crater and the mountains to the west. Next to the car park were the hotel and the waterslide that took people on a presumably terrifying ride that ended far below, in the lake water. Ivan half wished it was summer. Berenice sat with arms folded, engine running. Ivan and Cassie got out of the car. So did

Wilfred. He took the plastic shopping bags out of the boot and walked with Ivan and Cassie to the start of the road that led down into the crater.

"I'm sorry I can't help you more."

"You have helped us, a lot."

"I wish I could come with you."

The car horn beeped impatiently.

"You won't always be the youngest," said Cassie.

"You'll find better friends," said Ivan.

"I already have," said Wilfred.

"We should keep in touch," said Cassie.

Ivan wondered how.

"I'll give you my address. Maybe you can send a letter; you know, writing on a piece of paper—not a perso-text."

"I know what a letter is," said Cassie sadly.

Wilfred went back to the car and, ignoring whatever it was Berenice said to him (inaudible to Cassie and Ivan) found a piece of paper and a pen. He wrote on the paper and gave it to Cassie.

"Sorry about Mum. She can be changeable. She doesn't like people from Willowvale. Most people here don't. I like you, though. I've been trying to, um, keep her in the dark about that one. I'll put my perso-text number in too."

"Don't worry about your mum. I'm sure she loves you." Cassie folded the piece of paper and put it into her pocket. "Well, goodbye, Wilfred. I hope we meet again one day."

"Goodbye."

"Goodbye, then," said Ivan.

"See you," said Wilfred. He stood at the edge of the road and watched as Ivan and Cassie walked away. "I'll miss you. Be careful."

They stopped at the first bend and turned to wave. Wilfred was a silhouette on the edge of the crater. Berenice's car horn sounded impatiently, but Wilfred kept waving until they rounded the bend and he disappeared from sight.

The cold winter light cut through clear air making every detail of the scene sharp and close. Mountains shaped by blue shadows guarded the horizon as they always had. Nothing had changed about them. The crater with its barbaric size and violence, bare broken rock and harshly glittering water seemed to say to Ivan—even mountains lie. Didn't you know? Nothing is permanent, not even mountains. Nothing stays the same forever.

Ivan swapped his plastic bag to the other hand and looked back up at the resort hotel, perched precariously on the brink of the cliff above. He almost laughed out loud. It looked so fragile; the plastic tubes of the waterslide were like a child's crayon scribble on a wall, saying, *we were here*. Ivan thought the gesture rather sad. The earth could sneeze and be rid of the whole thing in a moment. Ivan smiled to himself and lengthened his stride to catch up with Cassie, who had her long dress hitched up over Berenice's jeans so she could walk fast.

They went down the winding road without talking for some minutes. Both looked back each time a bend brought the hotel into view, but they were too far away now to tell if Wilfred was still there.

CHAPTER 15
THE RIDGE AT SUNSET, AGAIN

Reenie was walking from school to Gran and Pop's place with Cal, to make sure that he'd settled in. That was the idea. His explanation of his predicament was confusing. "So tell me once more. I'm not stupid, it's that this is all so strange, it's hard to take it in."

"You're not stupid, Reenie. I can't take it in and it's happening to me. But I've worked out that the change happens at that exact place, near the poles. It happens exactly when the sun goes behind the hills, but only if the drums are playing at the same time."

"Well, getting back should be easy. Just be there. Go back—any time. Why don't you?"

"Can't you see?"

"What? Remember, I'm not stupid at all."

"The drums play every single sunset in my town, without fail. It's for the curfew, it's a rule. Here, they're random. I've been up there every afternoon I could since I worked it out. The drums here are sometimes too early, sometimes late. Lots of times they don't happen at all. It's impossible to predict. I can't get back any old time. Neither can Ivan get back here easily, even if he works it out. Ivan was up on the ridge at the right time the other day and I wasn't in the right place—he went, I didn't. Yesterday I wasn't there at the right time, but your dog came through from my side."

"You could wait for months for all those things to line up again, then."

"I know. But what choice do I have? There's no other way back."

Reenie had to let herself believe him. Today the whole far-fetched story that Cal told her, about the sunset and the drums and Ivan and some alternate Willowvale sounded preposterous, but Cal spoke so definitely. If she didn't believe him, she'd have to think he was completely mad, and that was not a good option. She thought again. "We could find out who's playing those drums and ask them to always play at sunset. That might make it easier."

"That hadn't occurred to me." They walked in silence for a while. The brief after-school traffic jam filled the street with a line of buses and cars. "But it could take ages to find the drummer here and persuade him or her to play at the same time each day. We'd have to knock on half the doors in town."

A bunch of older boys passed in a car, and yelled something that Reenie couldn't catch. Cal ignored them. "Aren't they your friends?" Reenie asked.

"Not really."

"Why do you go to school? You don't have to, nobody would even know about you, or how old you are."

"I thought I'd go crazy the first few days, not talking to a soul. It's mighty lonely when you don't know anyone. It was like that in O'Malley when I first went there too." Again, Reenie wondered in a corner of her mind whether Cal was just some weird kid spinning her a yarn. He went on, "Going to school's better than sitting on a rock all day, every day, waiting for sunset, believe me. And your school's a whole tree full of galahs better than school in my world. I've finished school there anyway. Have to find a job as a gardener or a blacksmith or something. If I go to school here I can still go up to the ridge every sunset; that's the important thing. I have to get back home, even if I don't want to now."

"You don't want to? I thought you did."

"Do and don't." Cal looked sideways at her.

"Look, if it doesn't work today, we can think about finding the drummer and asking them to play at sunset."

"Yeah, yeah." Cal shoved his hands down into his pockets and hunched himself over.

"We know the sound came from down the valley. It would only be a few streets," Reenie persisted. "We could ask around."

"And how are your parents today? How long can they wait?"

Cal had a point. Both her parents had spent every waking moment searching, asking, looking, talking to the police, to anyone. Both got up this morning looking ten years older than last week, as if they hadn't slept since Ivan disappeared, which was certain to be the truth. Reenie knew she had hardly slept, and that Anna had woken crying in the middle of every night, even last night when Mum let her take Frankie to sleep on her bed. The reassuring words of the police, that teenage runaways usually turned up within a few days, had done nothing to improve the way they felt.

"Do you think Ivan will come to any harm in your Willowvale? Think we can get him back easily now that we've got it all worked out?"

Cal grunted noncommittally. He looked at the sky. "It's not going to be obvious when the sun sets today. Look at those clouds."

"Think positive. It's not even four o'clock. Come on. If we don't find him, how can Mum and Dad? They think he's just run off or something, and even so, they're worried to death. Do you think anyone wants to be stuck in this situation? It's like a bad dream. I want to wake up and find I was asleep and everything's okay." Reenie was impatient with Cal's mood. School had been awful. Another day of people avoiding her because they didn't know what to say, if they knew her, or whispering about her if they didn't. Getting sent to the principal for slapping a horrible Year Nine boy. She'd hit him so hard across the face when he made a smart comment about Ivan that he'd had her handprint on his cheek for an hour. It was the highlight of the day.

"Sorry. You're right. Want an ice-cream or something?" said Cal. "Pass the time until sunset?"

"Haven't you got any studying to do?"

"Studying? You want to wreck my reputation? Anyway, I don't have any books."

"Who's paying for this ice-cream?" asked Reenie, knowing she was. For some reason, she didn't mind.

The afternoon seemed both long and short; both ordinary and strange. After the ice-creams they went to Reenie's house and played a childish, distracting game in the garden with Anna and Frankie. Cal carried in firewood and chatted with Gran while Reenie tried to concentrate on some homework. At last, after struggling unsuccessfully with an essay for too long, she looked out the window. The sun was sending coloured rays below the clouds. It would be easy to know when it set after all.

"It's getting late, Cal."

"Going out, darling?" Gran was reluctant to lose sight of anyone if she could help it, especially a child, even Cal who was not really a child, nor even related to her.

"Frankie needs a walk, Gran." Reenie hurried into her coat and a scarf and picked up Frankie's lead. Cal went to Gran and gave her a hug and a kiss. Gran laughed.

"Bye, Gran." Reenie kissed her too. "Gran will miss you when you go," she said to Cal as they headed for the top of the ridge.

"So will you," said Cal.

Reenie felt her breath catch in her chest. "What do you mean?"

"Oh, nothing. I thought you liked me, that's all." Cal's voice was less confident than a moment before.

Reenie felt her face redden. "I do like you. I will miss you," she mumbled.

"I guess I'll miss you too, then," said Cal, and smiled. He took Reenie's hand, and his hand felt warm and comfortable.

They walked in silence to the top of the ridge. The sun was a perfect circle of orange above the hills, roofed over by clouds, which reflected colour down onto the grey land. Cal went to the base of the poles and stood, waiting. He didn't look unbalanced, but he had the desolate look of loneliness that he'd had the day before, a look that was close to unbalanced in a quiet, sad way.

Reenie stood a little way off, near the rocks. She let Frankie wander about, sniffing trees and following wallaby tracks, never far away. "What if I never see you again? What if you can't find Ivan? What if he can't get back, after all?"

"Reenie, I'll find him," said Cal. "I'll send him back. Maybe I'll even come back myself, one day."

"He won't trust you," said Reenie, suddenly filled with dread that she'd never see either of them again. Why should Ivan trust Cal? And then, what if Cal was really crazy, and when the drums began, nothing happened. What if Ivan was lost somewhere in this real world, far from home, kidnapped, hurt, dead…but what if Cal wasn't crazy? What if when the drums played and the sun went behind the hill he did disappear into the other version of "here" that he talked about?

The drums began with a slow, ragged beat. The sun's rim touched the treetops across the valley. Reenie saw light seize Cal's hair like fire, and draw a line down his profile. "Wait!" She ran across the clearing to the base of the poles.

"Go back!" shouted Cal, "Reenie! Go back!" but Reenie grabbed his hand as the drums intensified and the sun seemed to fall behind the hills like a stone into water.

"Crumbling wombat shit, Reenie. You weren't meant to come with me."

"How do you know we've gone anywhere? We're still here."

"Yeah, but which 'here'? Do you know?" Cal spoke angrily.

"Here, there, it looks the same. I bet we're still in *my* here."

In answer, Cal took her hand, not gently, and led her to the edge of the rocky outcrop above the valley. "So where are all the lights of your 'here'?"

Okay. Reenie had to admit that there should have been lights in the valley, street lights and the dim glow of electric lights in distant windows. "Maybe there's a blackout."

"That'd be convenient. There's no blackout. What on earth are your parents going to do?"

"I'll be home in ten minutes, what do you mean?"

"No you won't, idiot. You're stuck here at least until tomorrow. What have you done?" There was a rustle in nearby bushes. Cal spun around to face toward it. "Shh. There's a psycho wombat around." He moved quietly toward the poles. "We'll go down the flying fox to my family's hut in the valley. It's safe there." Keeping one eye on the bushes, he said, "Climb up on the platform and find the handles—"

"Flying fox?"

"Believe me, there's a flying fox. It ends in the valley."

Reenie saw the spikes in the pole and a small platform that she'd never noticed before, a few metres from the ground. She climbed up. There was nothing that remotely resembled a handle of any sort. "There's no handle here. Nothing."

"Oh, no, Cassie must have forgotten to haul it up last time she used it. We'll have to run for it." Cal was silent for a few moments.

"We'll have to what? Let's go, it'll be dark soon. Let's go home."

"Shh. I'm listening for the wombat."

Both stood silently for a while. Reenie listened impatiently. She heard nothing but the slight movement of air among leaves and the distant call of a currawong—but something was wrong. Gradually she realized that there was no noise of trucks changing gear as they climbed the hill out of town, no traffic noise at all floating up to the ridge. Odd.

"I think we'd better go down the old road from the school, not through the gully to the valley. It's too steep, not a good track and it's getting dark. Follow me. Don't stop. The wombat won't chase us for long—but they can run pretty fast."

Reenie felt her heart beat faster despite the normal appearance of the scene. "What is this wombat? Wombats aren't dangerous."

"We have aggressive wombats here. Follow me—now."

Cal started fast as a wallaby across the backbone of the ridge and down the hill, jumping over rocks and fallen trees. Reenie decided she might as well follow. It would be silly to stand doing nothing. Making enough noise for a dozen wombats, she ran after him. It was difficult to see Cal; already he was a long way ahead. Reenie ran as fast as she could. Soon her lungs felt as if they were going to explode with cold evening air. "Cal! Wait!" she tried to yell. Gathering as much energy as she could, and wondering how she had lost the track, Reenie careered down the hill in what she hoped was the right direction. Surely there was a trail somewhere round here. She snatched a look behind her. No sign of a pursuing wombat, dangerous or not.

Reenie stopped. *I've got to catch my breath. Maybe I should go straight home right now.* Her heart thumped and her breaths were like the sound of a steam engine. She couldn't hear anything else. She climbed onto a nearby boulder to get her bearings. Was it safe to yell out to Cal? This was just the ordinary bush—there was no bloodthirsty wombat…Reenie looked around. Now that she was still, she recognized her location. Why had she imagined this was another world, even for a moment? Of course it wasn't. The streets that she'd always known were down there, just out of sight. Reenie took a big breath and shouted. "Cal! I'm going home! See you there. Gran will be getting worried." She whistled for Frankie. Frankie didn't come. Oh well, she must have run home already, hungry as usual.

Reenie looked down to jump off the rock.

Next thing she knew, she was lying face down on the ground next to the boulder, leaf litter pressing at her face, a heavy hand holding her down. She didn't have time or breath to scream.

"Who are you?" growled a voice. Reenie couldn't reply. The owner of the voice took in a sharp breath and the hand released its grip. "Is it you, girl? Cassie? Crumbling sandstone, I'm sorry." The hand picked Reenie up by the back of her jacket and she found herself standing unsteadily, half choked. The owner of the voice brushed her back roughly, yet apologetically. "Been on edge, sorry," he said.

Reenie turned slowly. Her assailant, or friend, was a very square shaped, quite young man dressed like a character from a Robin Hood film, with a bow and arrows and a dead rabbit draped over his shoulder. Reenie could do nothing but stare.

The man's apologies stuttered to silence. He stared for a moment then grabbed Reenie's arm. His hand was so large that he could grip around her upper arm as if it was a wrist. He started hurrying down the hill, dragging her with him.

"I don't know what the world's coming to. Not Cassie. Another mud-haired, skyeyed outsider. Look at her..." he gave Reenie a contemptuous look. "It's an—an epidem—an um, an epidem-istification. It's an invasion."

"Let me go!" Reenie got her voice in order at last. She tried to get free but the man's speed and strength prevented this. "Who are you? I'll call for the police. Help!"

The man didn't reply, but continued talking to himself, muttering darkly about strangers and the outside.

"Cal, where are you? Help!" yelled Reenie. "Help!"

"Got another with you, eh?" muttered the man. "I'd expect that." He gave Reenie's arm a shake and, reaching a potholed asphalt road, increased his speed down the hill.

"Cal, Cal," panted Reenie. Her feet tangled and she almost fell, but the man held her up by the elbow and continued along the road. "What are you doing? Where are you taking me?"

"Dunno. My place," said the man. Abruptly he turned from the road and into what looked in the fading light like the overgrown garden of a ruined house. Reenie couldn't remember any abandoned houses around here. A fire burned in the old brick chimney, throwing strange shadows out over the rough grass and straggly shrubs.

"John! John! Come here!"

CHAPTER 16
PIP RETURNS

"John! He's back! It's Pip!" called a young woman's voice.

The man dropped Reenie's arm and ran toward the fire. "Pip! I can't believe it."

Reenie staggered as John let her arm go, but regained her balance quickly. Who was Pip? There was excited conversation between John and the woman, exclamations of "How much you've grown!" and the reedy cry of a young baby.

Then Reenie heard Cal's voice. "We have to find my friend."

John's excited voice was suddenly quiet. Then he said, "I don't s'pose this friend is, um, a girl?"

"Yes, a girl. How did you know? I hope she's all right. What could have happened to her? I should have waited."

"There's a girl over there near the road. I found her in the bush. First I thought she was your sister. Then I thought she was an outsider. Didn't know what to do with her. Brought her here…"

Reenie sat down on the ground and put her hands over her face. She didn't feel like walking over to the fire and making them all feel less uncomfortable and guilty. She heard footsteps leave the fire and come across the garden, if it could be called a garden, crunching sticks and leaves. "Reenie? What are you doing out here?" She felt a hand on her shoulder; not John's heavy hand, but Cal's gentler one.

"Um…sorry, Reenie. I was so excited to be home, I guess I forgot to wait."

Reenie didn't think this apology deserved a reply.

"Come over by the fire," said Cal. "Meet John—"

"I've met him, thanks." She stayed put.

"He's all right. It was a mistake. Wasn't it, John?" In a louder voice, Cal repeated, "A mistake. A misunderstanding."

John grunted a reply which sounded like "Friendofyours?Sorry-girl," all rolled into one word.

Cal sat down by Reenie. "I really am sorry. Please forgive me."

Reenie kept her eyes shut under her hands. "This is your world, isn't it?" A whole night and day until she could even try to get home. It seemed like a long time.

"Come on, they're not so bad." Cal put his arm round her shoulders. "Come and warm up by the fire." Reenie got up, not looking at him, brushing his arm away. "Might as well make the most of it," said Cal. "My world, I mean. We'll find Ivan tonight and have him home by dinner time tomorrow."

John and his wife Jules seemed friendly enough. They were certainly happy to see Cal, or Pip as they called him. "Sit down, Pip, sit down. Rest for a bit. You must be tired, coming all that way. Have something to eat. Jules has cooked up a rabbit for tea tonight."

"Yes, you might as well stay for a bite to eat. The girl can stay too."

Cal sat down then stood up immediately. "Thanks, but we have to get going. I need to go home. It's a long time since I saw my parents and Cassie."

Reenie, in the shadows a bit away from the conversation, saw John and Jules exchange a worried glance.

"Didn't you know?"

"Know what?" Cal's voice was as worried as John's expression in the firelight.

"There's been bad trouble. Outsiders. They took your Cassie and a young fellow."

"Took them?"

Reenie felt her stomach swoop down inside her. She felt ill.

"Strange boy, dressed odd, like an outsider but not. Had a dog, funny little thing it was too. No brains, he didn't know as much as Isabel here." He gestured at the baby. "Said he was a friend of your parents…forget his name, Ian or something outlandish a bit like it…that's why I thought your friend was Cassie. Thought she'd come back with him."

"Where did they take them? When?" said Cal.

"Last night. Took them away on their smelly bike-machine things. Just drove up to the dance at the hall, threw them on the back and away with them in a noise like a tree falling into a hive of wasps—"

Cal jumped up. "We have to find them. Quickly."

"You can't run after them this time of night, Pip."

"My parents? Where are they?"

"Your mother left this morning after them. Gone to O'Malley, along with Mick Williams and Iris McPhee. Your dad's still here dealing with them in town. I think." John stirred the fire unnecessarily. "Big trouble in town. Bagshaw."

"We have to go." Cal was on his feet and heading for the street. "Come on, Reenie."

John and Jules insisted on accompanying them. This caused a short delay during which Cal paced restlessly, Reenie watched, and the others packed the dinner into a leather bag, raked out the fire and settled the baby into a sling arrangement made of an old blanket and leather straps.

"Hurry up, let's go," said Cal as Jules searched for her stick and John strapped a vicious looking knife to his belt.

Away from the fire it was not yet completely dark. Reenie felt in the rational part of herself that she should know where she was, but what she saw, walked through and smelt bore no relationship to what her brain said should have been there. She decided to convince herself that this was a completely new place. Cal had said he lived in Willowvale, they'd been in Willowvale as the sun went behind a hill, and he seemed to think they were still in the same place.

They walked for ten minutes along a rough road that passed nothing but trees, ruins and silence, and smelt of eucalyptus and frost. It was dark as they reached the top of a rise and met another road that joined the one they were on. The new road led down a long slope to a valley surrounded by dark hills below the darkening sky. At the bottom of the valley, in a bowl enclosed by the hills, was a town.

It was a small town, very compact. There were no lights. Reenie could see it by the smoke that rose from many chimneys and lay like a grey blanket over the roofs. John, Jules and Cal walked quickly. Reenie had to trot from time to time to keep up with them. She felt left out. The others didn't talk much, but when they did, it was not to her. Jules in particular gave out an air of disapproval, and though she waited once or twice, did it in a sighing, impatient manner that made it clear that she thought Reenie was in the way.

After twenty more minutes walking they came to a wall. It loomed dark above them, hiding the sky. There was a strong smell of horse manure in the night air, and smoke, and other fainter smells—rotting vegetables, sewage, and things Reenie couldn't identify. John led the way along a dirt path that followed the wall, in and out of bushes and around piles of junk, over a small creek that came out from a low stone culvert, and to another road.

The wall curved inward as it met the road. A large fortified gateway spanned the road where it entered the town. *We must be nearly there*, thought Reenie. Just then her foot caught in a twig and she fell to the ground. "Shh!" hissed John ahead and Jules from the rear. Cal helped her up. "There's a blackberry caught on my leg—"

"Shh."

"Who goes there?"

"What is this? A bad movie?" whispered Reenie to Cal.

Jules, from behind, put her hand over Reenie's mouth. "Shut it," she breathed. Even Isabel was quiet.

Cal took Reenie's hand. "It's okay, Jules, I'll look after her."

"Who's there?" said the voice again.

The group shrank back against the wall, behind a pile of rusty iron and other junk. Footsteps approached from the gateway, and Reenie saw a figure holding a burning torch, which was indeed exactly like a prop from a movie. The man waved the torch around, lighting nearby objects ineffectively with its yellow glow, grumbled something about possums and pigs, and went back the way he had come. She heard him muttering his way along the wall, and his voice faded as a gate clanged closed and a bolt was pushed into a slot. There was the sound of feet climbing wooden stairs, then silence. Cal bent down and untangled the blackberry stem from her ankle as if she was a small child, and took her hand again.

They waited for a long time. Reenie felt very cold as damp night air sank down into the creek bed. Cal kept a strong grip on her hand. Reenie was grateful that his hand was warm. At last John made a small signal and they began to walk stealthily beside the wall again. Fifty metres further they reached the main road.

The gate was in darkness, except for light coming from a modest watchtower at one side of the opening and a faint glow from inside the town. There was no traffic, and nobody to be seen. They crept closer, below the tower where a watcher would have had to crane out to see them, wary of any sign of movement in the lighted tower window.

John gestured with his arm and they dashed across the road where it entered the town through the closed gateway. Reenie didn't have time to look through the bars, and anyway, there was not much more light inside the town than out; she had an impression of crowdedness and a confusion of buildings inside.

Past the gateway they crept beside the wall for a few hundred metres, hiding behind bushes and piles of rubble to listen for the watchman—but there was no sound from him.

"John—it's near here," said Jules quietly.

"I know."

Behind the next bush, John fumbled with something set into the wall. There was a creaking sound and he opened a door. "Quickly. Once we're in and away from the door, they can't know we haven't been in all the time." Everyone squeezed through the small gap while John held the door, and then carefully closed it behind him. They were behind another bush.

"Anyone there?" whispered Jules.

Cal put his head round the edge of the bush and looked. "No."

"Hurry, then, out to the street, and straight to Raven and Thistle's place," said John.

Cal went around the bush, pulling Reenie behind him. "It's not far," he said.

They were in a laneway, one side contained by the wall, the other by shadowy fences. Cal led the way now, ducking into a narrow alley which was very dark, and came out into a quiet street. The smell of wood smoke was strong. Houses were black shapes either side, and there were no streetlights. A dog barked, then stopped. Cal walked faster than ever. Reenie clutched his hand now, uncertain of the ground she walked on, wary of tripping again, scared to speak. John and Jules walked behind. Isabel began to cry, a plaintive sound.

Cal turned a corner and led the way up another street, beside a tall paling fence—Reenie could hear the echoing of different air pressure as she passed, swooshswooshswoosh with each plank that was placed forward or back—then into another alleyway and at last to a wooden gate that creaked as Cal opened it with a key which he took from beneath a brick. "This is the back way," he whispered to Reenie. She couldn't see much, only the shapes of trees and closely built sheds in the yard. "Wait here," he said.

Reenie stood, swaying a little with sudden tiredness and the effort of balancing in the dark. John and Jules stood silently behind, and Isabel snuffled and gurgled quietly. Reenie's stomach rumbled. She could see the shape of a house across the garden. Cal disappeared down the dark path.

There was the clink of a chain, and a puzzled sound of a dog that has been woken. Cal whispered, "Quiet, Wolfie," and then Reenie heard the dog sniffing and licking Cal's hand, whining with excitement but controlled by what must have been excellent training. "Good dog," said Cal. "Come on, Reenie, it's okay."

Reenie felt her way along the path. The dog came up and sniffed her—she felt its nose on her hand. It was a big dog.

"Wolfie's all right," said Cal. He was already at the house, unlocking the back door. The dog pushed past Reenie, nearly knocking her down, to follow Cal's voice.

Nobody was home. The fire was faint coals in the old-fashioned kitchen fireplace; the end of one person's meal was cold on the table. "Raven—my dad—isn't here. We might as well eat while we decide what to do," said Cal. He rummaged in a cupboard and brought out some bread and a knife. Jules gave Isabel to John to hold while she unpacked the rabbit and cut it into rough chunks. Cal said nothing, stoking up the fire, filling cups with water from a tap outside. Reenie didn't know what to do so she fiddled around the table, arranging plates and cutlery that Cal brought out from drawers and shelves.

"Even Isabel knows to keep quiet near the watchman," said Jules in a deceptively conversational tone. Reenie wondered why Jules disliked her. She didn't say anything.

"She's never been here before. Lay off her," said Cal. "Take a look round the house," he said to Reenie in an awkward attempt at hospitality.

Reenie, glad to leave the kitchen, took a candle in a brass candlestick and wandered up the hall. She came to a room with an open door. It was a bedroom, dusty and disused-looking. She sat down on the bed. That was odd. Hanging on a wire coat hanger on the wardrobe door was Ivan's jacket. She put it on. So he had been here. She felt comforted.

Back in the kitchen, John had found a candle and lit it. They ate quickly and in silence. Reenie was glad she couldn't see the food properly, as it felt gristly and tasted unappealing—but she was hungry. Jules took the baby and sat feeding her in an armchair by the fire. John filled the kettle and searched for the teapot. "Think I'll stoke up the fire," he said.

"We can't sit around here all night, I've got to find Raven," said Cal.

"Calm down, Pip, Raven's old enough to look after himself."

"No. How can I?" Cal opened his mouth to say more when the dog began to bark.

A bell rang and someone shouted out from the lane. "Compulsory town meeting. I see your light. No exceptions. Town Hall. You're late."

"I'm not going. We've done enough," said Jules. "Blow out the candle when they go, John."

Cal said, "Do what you like. I'm going. Don't make yourselves too comfortable. Come on, Reenie." He slammed the door as they went out onto the veranda. The watchman's bell and shouts sounded along the lane. "We'll go round the front." He grabbed two knitted beanies from a hook by the door, gave one to Reenie, pulled his beanie down over his ears and led the way along the side of the house and into the front yard. He unlocked the gate. The large dog was on their heels. "Sit; stay, Wolfie." Cal locked the gate behind them.

They walked through dark streets. The occasional figure hurried along the footpath, going in the same direction. There were no cars or lights in the street.

"Who are John and Jules?"

"Oh, friends of the family."

"Is it safe to let them stay at your place? They seem a bit, um, a bit…" Reenie didn't know how to express the way she felt about John and Jules. "A bit unstable."

"I've got worse problems to worry about. So do you, for that matter."

They walked in silence for a moment, then Reenie couldn't resist asking more questions, despite Cal's terse answers. "What's this town meeting?"

"You'll find out. Keep a low profile, don't say a word. Don't attract attention. Crash course in Willowvale politics."

Reenie concentrated on her feet for a moment. *Willowvale politics? Did Willowvale have politics?* "Will the meeting be about getting your sister and Ivan back?"

"I doubt it—but we might find out some interesting stuff. They never decide anything much at these things, but…well, I want to go. Raven might be there already."

Reenie saw lights ahead at last. A row of burning torches like the one the watchman had held were tied to metal railings in front of a building that looked familiar. "That's the cinema. Is there a film on?"

"It's our town hall. Try to look inconspicuous."

Inside the hall was warm, stuffy and crowded with people sitting on old folding chairs and standing around the edges of the hall, leaning on the walls. The room was lit with candles and oil lamps. Several people sat at a table on a raised stage at the far end. A large, smartly dressed man stood in the centre of the stage in front of the table. Reenie and Cal squeezed into the back of the hall and stood there.

The large man was speaking. "This unfortunate event could

have a bad effect on our town." He had a loud, hectoring voice. Reenie felt angry, simply from his tone.

"Hear, hear," muttered scattered members of the crowd.

"We must stamp out the dissent that invites invasions like this." The crowd muttered uneasily, and there were one or two faint hear, hears.

"Nevertheless, we should send out a search party," someone said from the back of the hall. Cal started to turn toward the voice, then stopped himself and returned to a pose of indifferent attentiveness. Reenie tried to see where the words came from, but the faces of those around her were impassive, as if nobody had spoken. The last row of people up against the wall with them looked different from the rest of the crowd, and more than one person was so muffled with scarves and hats, despite the warmth of the room, that their faces were invisible.

"Who was that?" roared the man on the stage.

Nobody answered. The man on the stage went on. "If we are not united, if we let outside influences corrupt our society, we perish."

"If it was your daughter, you'd send a search party," said the interjector, not loudly, but audibly among the docile audience. People in the front of the hall craned their heads around. The back rows and those around the walls acted as if nothing had been said. Those on the stage stood up to look and the man in the centre puffed himself up like a rooster about to crow.

"I will not dignify this heckling with a response. I have issued an order. No search party. This is not a concern of ours. Those who venture outside the walls after curfew are outside our care. Any questions? This is a democracy. Any further remarks?" He peered aggressively into the crowd. Nobody spoke this time. "Mrs Bagshaw. Over to you. What is next on our agenda?

The meeting was long and boring. Reenie found herself falling asleep, even though she was standing up, leaning against the wall. Cal stood like a statue. The list of topics to be discussed seemed endless: order among school children, the threat from wombats, organizing a pig hunt, licences for trade through the gates, appointments to committees, changes to the bounty on cats. After what felt like hours, and a stream of tirades from the man who appeared to be the leader of the committee presiding from the stage, another man, who must have been the secretary, turned over the last page of his notes and folded them in front of him with a final-looking gesture.

"The main meeting is now closed. However we must continue with our bi-monthly issue of fines for infringements of rules," said the president.

'Fines for infringements of rules' was a very long segment of the meeting. There were many rules, and many people appeared to have broken them. Someone stood up with a list and read names and offences, together with the fines to be paid. Untidy front gardens. Allowing children to be disrespectful. Singing in public. Possession of a musical instrument. Frivolity. Reenie couldn't believe it. The perpetrators had to stand up and remain standing, until the whole list was read out. Reenie thought they were being treated like naughty children in an old-fashioned school.

"Is this a joke?" she whispered to Cal.

"Shh. I want to hear."

Most of the long piece of paper on which the list was written hung down over the top of the reader's hands. *This torture must be nearly ended.* She couldn't bear to see the people standing, waiting to be fined for growing too many chrysanthemums or for telling a joke. It was humiliating for her, and she wasn't even one of them. The reader ticked each offender's name on the paper then folded the list and put it on the table. "Report to the Committee after the meeting for your infringement notices and invoices." There was a general movement among the crowd as people stretched their legs in front of them and felt for coats, ready to leave.

"A moment please." It was the president who spoke. "There are some serious matters to deal with before anyone leaves. Recently there has been a slipping in standards. This must be dealt with." He brought another list from his jacket pocket. "Mick Williams, Penelope Williams, Iris McPhee. Reported outside town boundaries after curfew. Raven Rainhart. Thistle Redhill. Alleged possession of multiple illegal musical instruments. Outside town boundaries after curfew. Harbouring outsiders. Consorting with ferals. I want these offenders to be detained, please—doormen, stop them if they try to leave. These are extremely serious offences, and cannot be tolerated." His eyes raked the crowd. Cal sank down in his jacket and hat and Reenie saw his eyes search the back of the hall for a chance to leave. A woman further along did the same. "If these traitors to our town do not give themselves up, we will consider more serious action."

"I thought things might have improved while I was away," whispered Cal to Reenie. "But it's much worse. We'll have to go. No help here."

"They are not here?" said the president. "Take note—if they are in the hall, none of these people are to leave. They endanger our lifestyle. The rest of you may return to your homes. I issue a warrant for their interception. Meeting closed."

There was a general relieved movement toward the doors. A man with his face wrapped in a scarf stood up and left quickly from the end of the back row. Cal took off his leather jacket and held it bundled up under his arm. As they worked their way along the row of seats, Reenie saw a woman who had been sitting in the back row escorted away by two attendants. Another attendant stopped a man who had also been sitting nearby and started questioning him.

Cal hurried into the foyer and out into the crowd on the footpath, Reenie on his heels. "This is much worse than I expected. Much."

CHAPTER 17
THE OTHER WILLOWVALE

Reenie pushed through the crowd after Cal, who followed the man with the scarf as he threaded his way rapidly toward the darkness of the street. Suddenly a hand snatched Cal's knitted hat from his head. Cal's red hair flamed briefly in the flickering light as if it made light of its own, before Cal grabbed the hat back and pulled it down onto his head. Ignoring the intrusion, he looked around for the muffled man, spotted him as he crossed from the edge of the light into the darker street, and started through the crowd once more. Reenie was right on his heels as the hand caught Cal by the arm and brought him to an abrupt stop among the crowd, who were chatting sketchily to each other, keeping an eye over their shoulders.

"Well, well, Pip's back," said a voice which, like the hand, was bony and rough. Cal shook his arm free and looked toward the part of the night into which the muffled man had disappeared. Reenie shrank into a gap between two conversations. One of the conversations was between Gran and Pop, making the scene much more dreamlike. Reenie was glad Cal had warned her about them being in his world too. She listened. They sounded exactly the same as at home. "I knew those ferals would get Mick into trouble," Pop said, and Gran replied, "We'd better go and get Penny back," before Reenie tuned in to Cal's voice again.

"What's it to you?" Cal was saying.

The speaker, who was a tall girl about Cal's age, dressed in pastel colours, held the fabric of his shirt between her fingers as if she was thinking of buying it. "Everybody's missed you," she said. "'Specially me."

"Don't flatter yourself, Jess," said Cal.

Abruptly the girl's voice became less friendly. "It would interest our president to know that you're back. Very interested, he'd be, especially tonight."

Cal, twisting out of the girl's grasp, and said in a more polite tone, "Look, Jess, I'll catch up with you later. Got to go. I'll be around…"

Reenie saw his eyes flash in the lamplight, catch hers, and signal the direction he was taking. She pushed her way to the outside of the crowd and felt her way around the border between the people and empty street, where small groups broke off and walked away. *Where is Cal?* She couldn't see anything in the dimness, her eyes flickering with after-images of the fiery torches. She felt her way up the footpath for a few metres.

"Reenie! Let's go," Cal whispered from a doorway. Reenie jumped. Cal grabbed her hand and once more they were hurrying along a street contained by dark buildings and the delicate framework of deciduous trees. "We have to be quick."

"Who is that man you were following?"

"Still following. My father. Hurry."

"To your house?"

"I think he'll go to the shack outside town. Not safe at our house now."

"What about John and Jules? Will they be okay?"

"They're tough enough to look after themselves, believe me."

As they went, Reenie tried to reconcile her understanding of the layout of Willowvale with the place in which she found herself. "Isn't the shack in the valley down the creek? Aren't we heading towards your house now? It's the other way."

"Shh. The wall. That little door's the only easy way out at night. Hurry." Cal started to run through the darkness, pulling Reenie with him. "We must catch up with him."

Reenie still had many questions, but she had to use all her breath to keep up with Cal. She concentrated on keeping her footing. He took a route that changed whenever he saw other people, zigzagging around buildings and into back streets. Soon Reenie had lost all sense of direction, especially as the only light came from the candle-lamps of other pedestrians, who had to be avoided.

The further they went, the fewer people were on the streets as one by one each reached their home. Reenie saw the dark shape of the town wall ahead. Cal slowed and stopped in the deeper darkness beneath a tree.

"Okay," whispered Cal, "the door is just over there—see the big bush?" Reenie couldn't see it. "We'll have to be careful here—someone might be watching." Keeping close to fences they continued quietly until, black against the bulk of the wall, Reenie saw the bush that concealed the door. They drew up behind a protruding garden wall and listened. Silence.

"All clear," said Cal. They started toward the bush, which extended out over the dirt footpath. As they reached its spiky edge, a voice broke into the night air.

"Stop! No-one passes."

Both froze. Another man's voice came through the bush. "It's an emergency. I have to go out of town."

"Raven. You know Mr Bagshaw has ordered your arrest. "

Raven laughed. "Huh. That puffed-up bag of barnyard feathers."

"Is that your father?"

"Shh."

"Come on, Gary. Stop this. Let me out. You know I don't believe in violence."

Despite this statement, sounds of struggle came raggedly through the bush.

"Guards! Guards! Support! Guards!"

"Let me go."

"You're leaving town clandestinely during curfew. It's a breach of the regulations. There are orders—"

"It's definitely him. I'll distract the guard. You run for the doorway, grab Raven, get him outside…" Cal whispered. He bent down and picked up a rock from near the base of the wall and threw it out into the laneway, where it fell with a thud.

"Who's there?" called the guard.

Cal picked up a broken piece of concrete and threw it the same way.

"Who is it?"

"He's not coming. Call out 'Help' or something."

Reenie remembered someone once telling her to yell 'Fire!' to get attention. "Fire!" she screamed. "Fire! Help!"

"Let me go, you fool, someone is in trouble," said Cal's father.

Reenie didn't hear the guard's reply.

"You'd better check, it sounds serious. I'll wait."

"Really?" The guard's voice was loud with astonishment.

"I give you my word. You know me, Gary."

Cal had crept in an arc across the lane and back to the wall at the far side of the doorway. "Help!" he cried in a high-pitched voice. The guard's footsteps went that way. Reenie waited a few seconds, then "Fire!" she yelled and the guard's steps came toward her. Before the guard reached her Cal's voice came again, and when the guard's steps went that way Reenie hurried to the door. Cal shouted again, leading the guard away. Not too far away, she hoped.

"Mr Raven! Come with me. I'm a friend of Cal's—of Pip's—let's go."

Cal's father didn't move as Reenie tried to urge him through the door. "I said I'd wait for Gary," he said, then, "What are you saying? Pip? Who are you?"

"Pip is here. Hurry."

"I don't believe you."

"Help—this way—" Cal's voice was farther away. The grumbling voice of the guard was still audible, following.

"That's him over there, distracting the guard. We're here to save you."

"I don't need saving. And who are you? How do I know you're not lying? Pip's been missing for a year. He's not here."

Reenie remembered that Cal was sure Ivan had met his parents and been helped by them. "I'm Ivan's sister. I'm from the other Willowvale, where Ivan came from. Cal—I mean Pip—is my friend there. He's back. I've come to get Ivan—"

The sounds made by Cal and the guard had faded. No other guards had appeared yet.

"Come on, Mr Raven, Cal will catch up with us."

"He told you his real name?"

"Can we go? We have to find Ivan and your daughter; we can't if you're arrested."

"I know that. But I promised Gary."

Reenie thought this strange Willowvale was filled with very odd people, and racked her brain for another argument. Running feet approached and Cal burst around the bush, nearly knocking her over.

"Come on Reenie, hello Raven, let's go."

"Pip?"

"Yeah, it's me. Can we get a move on?"

"Stop! Guards!" Gary was not far away.

"Come *on*..."

Cal's father didn't move. "I told Gary I'd stay."

Cal groaned. "He's a guard. It doesn't matter what you told him."

"Get yourselves out. I can deal with him, Pip." Raven's voice was stern.

"Raven!" Gary was very close now, and panicky.

Raven hustled Cal and Reenie through the doorway. "Go. I'll find you."

Gary panted up to the doorway. "Raven. You're still here."

"I gave my word," said Raven. Then at once, his voice became persuasive. "Now, Gary, you know how important it is for me to find Cassie. Rex Bagshaw has gone too far these last few months. Everyone knows it. So I'm going, and you're not about to stop me, are you?"

"I know, Raven, I know, but it'll cost me my job if I let you go."

"This whole town's built on lies. You know that. Tell a few yourself. Tell Rex you never saw me, tell him I overpowered you, tell him anything you like. Imagine if your daughter was the one missing. Just think about it. Imagine if it was Tracey."

Cal and Reenie were pressed against the wall nearby, listening with their breath caught in their throats.

"Will he let him go?"

"I don't know. Shh."

Gary's voice was troubled. "I am imagining if it was my daughter. Even so, I'm not sure I can deal with Mr Bagshaw."

Raven sounded impatient. "He's a bully. Talk to him in his own language. Shout at him in his own language. He lies so much he doesn't expect anyone else to. He'll believe you, I know it. I have to go."

Leaving Gary standing in surprised silence, Raven walked through the door as calmly as if he was going to have a look at the stars from his front veranda. He walked along the track outside the walls until he came to the place where Reenie and Cal waited.

"Raven."

"Pip. You are back. It really is you." They embraced. "We'd

better move on. Gary won't stand around pretending to guard the door for long. Soon he'll start wondering what happened to those strange people who were calling for help." His voice had a smile in it. "We've got a lot to do. Your mother's gone after Cassie already. I stayed to get some help but there's none in this town."

"So it is true? Cassie's been taken by outsiders?"

"I'm afraid so. And a boy—" Raven paused. "Ivan. I'm confused. There was a girl back there, said she's his sister. They took Ivan too. Where's the girl got to?"

"She's here. This is her, Reenie." Cal pushed Reenie forward to shake hands with Raven in the dark.

"That's just what we need." Raven sounded like a person who didn't want to consider any more complications. He also sounded as though he was trying by an act of will to postpone his joy at finding Cal until a more convenient moment. While the conversation continued they walked along the perimeter track outside the walls. "Thistle, Mick and Iris left for O'Malley this morning to find Cassie and Ivan. They had horses. It's going to take them at least two days to get there. We had no way of getting more horses or a vehicle in this place the way things are. I could kick myself, wasting time waiting for that ridiculous town meeting. I should have known better. By basalt, Bagshaw even took Penny Williams for questioning. He's really gone too far."

"Raven—"

"I was hoping to get together a search party, but Bagshaw has turned into a little despot, and barely a soul will stand up to him." Raven walked faster than John and Jules, so that even Cal had to trot to keep up.

"Yes, I saw it. We were at the meeting. Raven—"

"Shush."

They came to the main town gates. A group of guards stood talking inside the bars, a bonfire in the road sending rays of light onto the road outside. Raven hardly altered his gait, but took a wide detour away from the light, tracing the darkness back to the wall near the place where Reenie, Cal, Jo, John and the baby had crossed the small stream that emerged from the town.

Cal tried again to speak. "Raven, I—"

"We'll go along the creek," said Raven, and led the way down the bank of the stream, paying no attention to mud and wet feet.

Reenie did her best to keep up, but Cal noticed that she lagged behind. "Wait a minute," he said. Raven paused. Cal took Reenie's hand. "Raven, can you listen to me for just a few seconds?"

"Sorry, Pip, I am overwrought. I should be asking you what happened to you, where you've been. Of course I'm happy to have you back it's not a good time for talking—"

"Not that. I've got a bike. A motorbike. I can get to O'Malley in a few hours. I can find them."

For the first time Raven stopped and gave Cal his full attention.

"You have a motorbike? Fuel?"

"It's hidden up on the ridge. Fuel—not much—is there any way of getting some?"

"We'll go straight away. I think I can borrow fuel."

"We?"

"You and me."

"What about Reenie?"

Raven had forgotten Reenie. She knew it. "We'll get fuel," he said carefully, "and then we'll work out what to do. We'll have to go back into town." He turned and they retraced their steps along the creek. "This way," said Raven, and he bent and started to crawl into the culvert that brought the water underneath the wall.

By the time they'd obtained a stolen—or "borrowed", as Raven insisted—jerry-can of fuel from a shed full of skeletons of machinery that tried their best to break everyone's shin bones, Reenie thought she would never be warm again. The town was quiet now, except for the guards at the gates. They discussed using the door guarded by Gary, but that was a long way round, and Gary might not be so co-operative a second time. There were sure to be guards at all the gates. The culvert was the only way out, and that meant crawling through water and mud in the stone tunnel. By the time they were outside the wall again, Reenie couldn't stop shivering. They started walking away from the town; soon, Raven stopped.

"Now we can plan. Where is this motor bike?"

"It's hidden up on the ridge, but Raven, I think—"

Reenie started to think that Cal may have run away from home because he was tired of being interrupted. "There's no time to waste, Pip, don't waste words either," said Raven.

"Raven, listen to me. We can go in the morning. I know the bike riders. I know where they go, I know what they do. I was with them most of the time I was away. Can you please listen to me? Look at Reenie." This was not a logical request, given the darkness, but there was a silence long enough for Raven to hear Reenie's teeth chattering. "We're all soaked. We haven't eaten for hours. I'm…fairly…sure Cassie and Ivan will be okay…outsiders aren't as bad as people think. A few hours won't make much difference, not if we've got a bike. Let's go to the shack and do this properly, not kill Reenie with hypothermia."

Reenie was surprised to feel Raven's hand on her forehead. He didn't speak for a moment, then said, "I'm sorry."

"Do you think the committee will send their people to the shack, looking for you?"

"The town committee is all bark and no real bite. They won't come now."

"Gary won't say anything?"

"I don't think so. Does anyone know you're here?"

"Only John and Jules."

Reenie decided it was her turn to speak. "And that horrible girl outside the meeting. How far is it to the shack, then?"

"I wish we had the dogs with us," said Raven. "I hope Wolfie will be all right. We left Magda with Charlie and Marg Williams. What will Thistle say when she sees you, Pip?"

"Probably, 'Do you know how much trouble you've caused?'" joked Cal. "And don't worry about Wolfie, John and Jules and Isabel are staying at the house."

Raven sighed. "Well I hope they don't eat us out of house and home or burn the place down. And that they have the sense to feed the dog."

It took half an hour to reach the shack. Dazed with cold, Reenie hardly noticed walking there. She stumbled the last few dozen metres up the steep path, and leaned gratefully on Cal while Raven unlocked the door. She was asleep under moth-eaten kangaroo-skin rugs and old woollen blankets in a corner, before Raven and Cal had lit the fire, and when Cal brought her a cup of black tea and a piece of damper, he couldn't wake her. She didn't hear the conversation between the father and son that went on into the night, but it didn't concern her. They had a lot to catch up on.

CHAPTER 18
WALKING TO WILLOWVALE

Ivan and Cassie settled into an uneven rhythm, following the road up and over ribs of scree that leaned, stone balanced uncertainly on stone, from the crumbly top edge of the crater down to the water's edge. The lake was smaller than it had seemed in the night, however, it was large enough that it took Ivan and Cassie nearly an hour to walk from the last of the shut-up resort buildings to the point where the track started to ascend the far wall of the crater.

Cassie walked at a rapid pace. Ivan, shifting his plastic bag from one hand to the other, made an effort to keep up as she ascended the crater wall. The gradient was steeper and the drop from the edge of the road more precipitous than Ivan had realized when they travelled down the stretch two nights before. Cassie slowed as she climbed, but even so, Ivan strained to catch up until they reached the straight section below the last hairpin bend. Cassie stopped. Ivan didn't want to. He glanced at the pile of rocks that marked his landing from that terrible fall in the dark, and continued to the top without a word. They paused there to catch their breath. The hotel and waterslide were mere coloured squiggles on the far cliff.

"I wonder if we'll ever see Wilfred again," said Cassie.

Ivan didn't know, and said nothing. The road stretched ahead of them in the familiar yet not familiar way that in itself was becoming normal to him; it was a ragged version of the road he saw from the car on every trip to O'Malley. The hills and mountains all around were as he'd always seen them, and for a while he walked looking only at the scenery and thinking of nothing but the shape of the road under his feet and the hills against the sky. Despite the scenery, however, it was impossible to ignore the old tree trunks lying on the ground beneath newer growth: all of them fallen away from the impact in the crater, exactly as Aunty had described.

They were some kilometres past the crater lake when the realization Ivan had put aside earlier came to the front of his consciousness as unwelcome as a bunch of gate crashers at a party. Phil. How could Ivan explain—what would he tell Cassie about Phil? Should he tell her anything? Her heroic lost brother...he didn't want to spoil her illusion. As Ivan walked these thoughts tossed about in his head so that he could almost feel them battering at the inside of his skull.

Cassie turned and looked at Ivan, as if she knew he had something to say. This caused Ivan to blurt out the first thing that occurred to him, though not the thing that most concerned him.

"Tell me more about Willowvale."

"Never mind that. I just remembered. You said something about knowing Pip—"

"I'm really interested in your world, we've got hours to talk in. How about you tell me—"

"Forget 'my' world. It's *the* world. You tell me something—"

This felt like the worst ever game of Truth, Dare and Double Dare.

Cassie, for once, didn't press for a reply, but walked silently for several minutes, fiddling with the velvet of her long skirt.

Ivan tried to go back to thinking blank kinds of thoughts about his feet hitting the ground one after the other, and whether he should change hands with his plastic bag, and how far they'd walked; but he couldn't. He took a quick sideways glance at Cassie and caught her doing the same at him. He quickly lowered his gaze. He wished he was the one asking the questions.

"Tell me about the traders, the—"

"You said you knew Pip when you saw the photo. Don't say you didn't," said Cassie, speaking over Ivan.

"Um,"

"You did. You said you know him. You said it more than once. You said he's in your Willowvale. Tell me about it. Why did it take so long for you to work it out?"

Ivan sighed. "I recognized him when I saw the photo. Before that I didn't know they were the same person. Yes, I know him. Sort of."

"Why didn't you work it out for so long? Is Pip a common name in your world?"

"No, I never met anyone called Pip. It's an old-fashioned name, I think, nobody much has it…you know how many names your brother used in O'Malley. He has a different name in my Willowvale."

"Radcliffe, then? Is that what he calls himself there?"

"That's a surname, not a first name. Or if it is, I never heard it. He calls himself Phil at home."

"So you realized when you saw the name in the café?"

"I recognized his face."

"You two are friends! It's wonderful. It makes things so much easier," said Cassie happily. She held her skirt out and twirled in the middle of the road.

Ivan sighed again. "Look, Cassie, we're not friends. He hates me."

"Don't be stupid. Of course he doesn't. Pip's not like that."

"How would you know? I'm telling you. You aren't me."

"But Pip's not that type of person."

"How long is it since you saw him? A year?" Ivan tried to walk ahead, but Cassie easily kept pace with him. "Don't you think people can change? Even if he was the perfect brother, or the perfect person, before, he's not like that now."

"What do you mean?"

Ivan paused to put his words into an order that would not hurt Cassie. He spoke slowly, to make time to think. "You know those kids we met in O'Malley, the ones that weren't real friends of Wilfred's?"

"Yes."

"If—if you asked me to think of someone like that in my life, it would be Phil. Pip."

"You're wrong. Maybe the Phil you know is a completely different person. Maybe it's not him."

"Cassie, I'm kicking myself that I didn't realize earlier. Phil can't possibly be someone else. He's your brother. Pip. Radcliffe. Phil. All one. He appeared out of nowhere."

"But why would he be a—a horrible person in your world? He's not like that when he's here."

"Well, why did he run away? Maybe he wasn't as perfect—" Ivan changed his word when he saw Cassie's hurt expression—"as good, as happy, all the time, as you think. Everyone has their faults— Cassie, I am telling the truth."

"But how do you know it's him?"

"He looks exactly like the photo. Except for the clothes, of course. He has a leather jacket like this." Ivan flapped the jacket he wore to emphasise his point. "Exactly like this. There are no jackets the same in my world, except that one. He's got hair like you but darker, a face like you, the same eyes; he even walks like you. It's impossible that he isn't your brother. I just didn't think of it before because so much was happening."

Cassie didn't say anything. She changed her plastic bag to the other hand and kicked a stone along the road.

"Cassie. Even if he's not my best friend—and I did like him

when he first came—I'm helping you get him back, aren't I? It doesn't matter if I like your brother or not."

Cassie wiped her hand across her nose and nodded. "I understand."

"I feel extremely stupid that I didn't realize you were related as soon as I saw you. I mean, the last person I saw before I came here was him—" Ivan stopped in mid-sentence.

"What's up?"

Ivan took a deep breath as he remembered that moment. "I was up on the ridge—you know, where I met you—I was reading. Phil—your brother—Pip—came along, running as if his life depended on it, and he yelled at me. He was furious. I thought it was his usual sh— um, stuff, the way he picks on me."

Cassie was silent.

Ivan strained to bring that confused moment back to life. "He was running. I was at the poles. He yelled at me to go away. Then suddenly I was here, and I didn't see him again. I saw you."

"He'd worked out how to get back here, then," said Cassie flatly. "You came, and he stayed."

"Yes." Ivan felt flat as Cassie's voice sounded. "So I suppose you're going to say it would have been better if he'd come and I'd stayed back home."

"No." Cassie bounced as she walked. Suddenly she was happy.

Ivan was surprised.

"It's obvious. If Pip was in your world—how long was he there for?"

"A few weeks, a month maybe."

"He would have worked out how to get back just before, or when you came here. That's the only reason he was angry. You were in the way. You were at the poles at sunset, and he wanted to be there."

"He was angry all the time, not only then."

"Yes, but think about it. He must have, you know, crossed over to your world by mistake, when he was on his way home to us! That's why he was angry. Wouldn't you be? He was disappointed. The motorbike mechanic in O'Malley said he wanted to come home. Remember? Aunty did too. So he went to Willowvale, my Willowvale, and got to yours by mistake. He was stuck there for a while and now he's worked out how to get home. Pip'll get here. He could be here already!" She paused for breath, then went on, "And for your information, Ivan, I'm really glad we met. Do you think I have a lot of friends at home? Do you?"

Ivan thought about the incident with Wilfred's 'friends' in O'Malley. Hadn't Cassie said she knew people like that, too? He remembered the people in Willowvale staring not only at him, but also at Cassie and her parents—unfriendly stares. "So I'm your friend?"

Cassie stopped on the road and thumped Ivan on the arm. "Of course you are. Other than Pip, you're my best friend in the whole world. And Wilfred, too, of course. He's my other best friend. Yours too, I bet."

Ivan agreed. Wilfred was a good friend, whether they saw him again or not. "Don't you have any friends at home?" he asked, not wanting to admit to the warm feeling Cassie's speech gave him.

"They're all like those kids in O'Malley. They call me names, pretend to be nice when they're being horrible. They tell tales behind my back—they never get caught by an adult—and anyway most adults wouldn't care. Pip had friends, but I never did. And they didn't seem to care much when he ran away. Maybe they weren't real friends to him after all."

"Why do you think he ran away?"

"He got in a sort of gang with some of the town kids not long before he left. He used to hang around with them all the time. I didn't like them, and they didn't take any notice of me. I think the arguments he had with our parents were about them."

Ivan thought that Phil probably would get on best with those kinds of kids, but said nothing.

"Then he got into some kind of trouble. I don't really know what it was. There was going to be a town meeting. Do you have town meetings?"

Ivan shook his head.

"All this time, Pip was...I don't know. He changed. He was different. He was the same as ever to me, but he had a few—a lot...of...arguments—with Thistle and Raven before he disappeared. I didn't think that was enough to run away over, though. Everyone has arguments."

Ivan reached across and held Cassie's hand. They walked in companionable silence for a long time. The sun moved behind them, closer to the mountains. Currawongs started their afternoon carols to the sun. White cockatoos flapped in trees like animated blossoms. *How*, thought Ivan, *can life be so difficult and so wonderful at the same time?*

CHAPTER 19
REENIE AND CAL RIDING

"No," said Raven, as they hiked through the morning mist to fetch Cal's motorbike from its hiding place. "We can't leave you alone here. It's not reasonable. I'll get hold of a horse and follow as quickly as I can. You must go with Pip."

He was so calm. Reenie wanted to ask him so many things; how he felt about having Cal back, for instance, but Raven was different from anyone Reenie knew, and he did not seem the kind of person to be asked strings of questions. Reenie was glad of the woolly scarf and hat. She pulled her jacket closer around her and Cal's woolly hat down over her ears and was glad she'd thrown the jacket on as she left the house when she left home. It seemed so long ago. At least she felt better than last night. She couldn't remember going to sleep in the hut. When she woke, Cal and Raven had already made porridge for breakfast, tasteless and chewy but filling. They ate quickly and left in the dim pre-dawn twilight. Reenie wanted to have a good look at the hut, and work out exactly where it was. She thought it was in the same place as her friend Sarah's house, but she wasn't sure. The world was swathed in mist.

The fog made everything beautiful and mysterious in the early light. Despite the strangeness, Reenie enjoyed walking with Cal and Raven. Fog was frozen onto spider webs and grass seeds so that they were white with tiny crystals of ice.

Cal led the way past the poles, which loomed out of the mist above the steep gully track. They continued some distance, going away from the town, along the ridge to a rocky outcrop in an area that Reenie had not explored. Cal jumped down behind a projecting rock and began throwing aside fallen branches still rustling with stiff leaves. Soon Reenie saw a shiny handlebar and the complicated front section of a motorbike. Raven climbed down beside Cal. They uncovered the petrol tank and seat, threw a helmet up to Reenie, who caught it awkwardly and shook dry leaves and dead spiders out of it. Without a word, Cal and Raven pushed the bike out onto the hillside. Reenie followed them as they wheeled it up the hill toward the faint track that ran along the ridge. The motorbike looked like an alien creature shining and red, sharp edged and heavy in this setting of pale indeterminate shapes and colours, the mist transforming everything else to fit its floating opalescent world.

Reenie, staring at two trees that made a doorway, and wondering if she walked through it would she be somewhere else, suddenly realised that the others had reached the track and roused herself to catch up with them.

"We can't start the bike here. It'll wake the whole town."

They wheeled the bike along the track, carefully pushing it over the crest of the ridge and down the far side, which was gentler in slope and surface. Reenie thought she recognized the route now, an old fire trail that in her Willowvale led to the last streets of the town, where back yards blended with the bush on the ridge and the paddocks and small acreages lower down. She looked across in the direction of home. *No. It's not there; don't be silly*, she thought, but couldn't prevent herself stopping anyway, searching with ears, eyes and nose for a faint trace of her family and home. Nothing. No wood smoke nearby, no dogs barking, no rooftops through the trees.

Cal and Raven stopped a little ahead at the point where the trail faded out of the trees and disappeared into wispy grassland. Reenie heard snatches of words. She moved closer, forcing herself to abandon the temptation to run for home. Raven and Cal were pouring petrol from the jerry-can into the bike's tank, and pressing the tyres with their thumbs to check the air pressure.

"I'll leave you here. I have to get hold of a horse before the day gets too old," said Raven, as Reenie approached. "Be careful, you know who lives over there." He gestured over the next hill, where, if this was her Willowvale, Reenie knew were large houses on small acreages.

"Are you sure you don't want me to stay here? I'll be okay," Reenie said, but Raven, not listening, was hugging Cal like a bear, kissing him on the forehead. He surprised Reenie by doing the same to her. "Don't worry about me. Be strong. You'll find them." He walked with long strides into the fog.

Cal put the jerry-can carefully behind a fallen log. "You can have the helmet," he said, and set himself on the bike seat, adjusting the rear vision mirror and testing the brake levers. He took a key on a chain from his neck. Reenie, watching, had a flashing thought that he was the most beautiful creature she had ever seen. Pushing this thought aside she fumbled the helmet onto her head, her face as red inside it as the enamel on its exterior.

"Hop up, then," said Cal. He put the key into the ignition. Reenie climbed onto the seat and sat with her hands braced behind. "No, stupid. Sorry. I mean, that's not safe. Hang onto me." He turned the key as Reenie carefully put her arms around him. The engine coughed. Cal laughed.

"What's funny? That engine sounds bad."

Cal turned the key again and the engine roared into action. "Just happy," Reenie thought he said, but she wasn't sure. "Hang on." He turned the throttle and the engine revved. The bike began to move.

For the first ten minutes of the ride, Reenie kept her eyes tightly shut while she held so closely to Cal that each of her hands reached to the other elbow. *What would Mum and Dad say about riding a motor-*

bike, she wondered briefly, then realized that would pale into insignificance in relation to what they knew she had done: disappeared into the night. With a strange man. And all on top of Ivan being lost for three nights. There was nothing to be achieved by worrying about her parents, though, and she could do more by staying on the bike with Cal, finding Ivan, and getting home safe and sound. Cal wasn't a stranger now, anyway. Reenie closed up the space in her head called 'Worrying about the family' and set her mind to 'Not being scared' and 'Finding Ivan'.

It was cold on the motorbike, even behind Cal who deflected the wind. There was no point trying to speak over the rushing air and engine noise, no matter how much she wanted to ask questions, or apologize for being here, taking Raven's place. But that was a regret from the 'Reenie is too polite' part of her brain. She tried to dismiss it. There was no asking questions nor hearing answers to be done now, though Reenie's mind was so full of questions that she didn't pay attention to the road that disappeared into the fog as soon as they found it and faded into nothing a hundred metres ahead. After a while Cal brought the bike to walking pace and pulled off the road. The wind ceased. There was no real wind, it was only their own motion that made Reenie feel the movement of the air.

"You can hop off for a minute," said Cal as he cut the engine.

"Why are we stopping?"

"Shh. Listen."

Reenie took the helmet off so that she could hear better. Her ears still echoed engine noise. She tried to listen but could hear nothing. "What are we listening for?"

"Shh. Engines. Trucks."

Again there was an interval where Reenie heard nothing but her own heart beating. Perhaps she even imagined that.

"What truck are we listening for? I didn't think you had trucks."

"There's one that goes up to O'Malley every day. Bagshaw's

business. He's the only one who's allowed to trade. And if Jess told him she saw me last night, he'll be after us for sure. I don't want him to catch up with us. They might be on the truck."

"Who is Bagshaw?"

"You were there last night. Bagshaw. The town president."

Reenie remembered the meeting and the ugly arrogance of the man in charge of it. This information left her silent, and into this silence came the distant sound of an approaching vehicle.

As they listened to the engine, Reenie pictured the strange girl who spoke to Cal outside the meeting. The memory of her had niggled; her arrogance and malice was very like Bagshaw's, now that she knew of their relationship. "Was that Jess who threatened you last night?" Reenie was just as curious about Jess as she was sure they should stay ahead of the truck. "She sounded unbalanced. Is there something wrong with her?"

"You saw her last night? Lucky she didn't see you. She used to be my friend. We were in a group, you know, like a gang."

"She seemed to think you were her...um...was she your girlfriend?" The fog magnified the strangeness of the situation. At that moment it hid Cal's face although he was very close. This odd unreality made Reenie ask a question she would not otherwise have asked. The question might give the wrong impression...if only she knew what the wrong impression was.

The truck engine changed note as the driver shifted gears. Cal was suddenly alert, like a small animal that knows a predator is nearby. He put his hand on Reenie's arm and pointed to some trees and bushes that bordered the area where they had stopped. Reenie followed as he wheeled the bike behind a bush, past a dead campfire in a ring of stones.

"We'll hide."

"I think we should go. There's still time. There's no reason to hang around here."

"Shh."

"They're a long way off, Cal. We've got time to get away."

"Yes, I know. Sorry. I'm jumpy after last night."

"Why did you stop here? It would be better to stay ahead of this truck."

"I don't want to get mixed up with them. They all work for Bagshaw. I want to keep away from them…" His voice faded to nothing.

"But if they get ahead of us, they'll find your mother and the others before we do. That would be a disaster." Reenie took hold of the handlebars of the bike and said again, "We need to stay ahead of the truck. Think about it, Cal."

The sound of the approaching engine floated through the invisible landscape. A currawong called into the whiteness as it flew past, its wings tearing the mist. "I need to tell you something, Reenie," said Cal. "Jess wasn't my girlfriend. She just wanted to be. If I had a girlfriend I'd want one like—"

"Not that it's my business," said Reenie quickly.

"She's like her parents, thinks everything belongs to her and she can just take it, especially since her father got to be town president. He started really throwing his weight around and so did she. I sort of realized that there was something wrong in Willowvale then, and things got bad with Jess then too."

"What do you mean? Can you please get on the bike? We have to go."

"Life had been pretty restricted before, but it got a lot worse when Bagshaw got to be president a couple of years ago. I began to realize that the things my parents said were true."

"So it hasn't always been like a prison camp there?" Reenie couldn't get onto the pillion seat unless Cal was in his seat. She shook the handlebars. "Come on, Cal."

"We learnt history at school, but nothing about before the

disaster. I thought Thistle and Raven were just complaining, talking about the good old days and what life was like before, you know how parents do…but I saw some of the things that went on when I was Jess'…friend, and it made me think. Maybe my parents were right."

"What things?" asked Reenie in spite of her impatience.

"You saw the town. Does it look like a fun place to live? Lots of food, easy life, opportunities for everyone?"

"It was dark, Cal. What would I know? Now can we go, please?"

"Does Willowvale seem like a fun place to live?" Cal persisted. "Tell me, Reenie." His face was right near hers.

"No, of course not."

"Well, what if I told you that the Bagshaws live in a huge mansion out of town, with a car like the ones in O'Malley or in your world, and an electric generator, and all sorts of stuff from the city: fancy food, carpets, music playing machines—when if anyone else hums in the street or paints their fence yellow they get fined or worse? And that the Bagshaws and their cronies pretend that O'Malley or anywhere outside Willowvale is a dangerous place, too dangerous for ordinary people to see? And they make everyone scared of everything, until they'll do what they're told?" Cal was speaking fast.

Reenie wanted to listen, but she wanted to go, too. "Do they?" She shook the handlebars in frustration.

Cal grabbed Reenie's arm and shook it just as hard. "Tell me. What would you think? You saw our house. It's nothing much. You saw the wall and the guard post, and the truck stable, and the shack. You were at the town meeting, for granite's sake. Do you think everyone in Willowvale has what Bagshaw has?"

"So…are you saying that Mr Bagshaw stops everyone else from doing things then does it all himself anyway? Travelling to O'Malley, getting new things, stuff like that?"

"Yes. And when I was friends with Jess, I found out about all that, and I suddenly felt sick at the thought of the place I'd lived nearly all my life. I couldn't stand it. I tried to get Jess to understand, to persuade her father to change how he ran the town."

"Ambitious," said Reenie shortly, nearly exploding with the wish to get away before it was too late.

"Yeah, stupid, you mean. She made all the kids I thought were my friends hate me. They made my life a misery, and it started to come back onto my parents and Cassie too. Things got much worse. I couldn't stand it."

"So you ran away."

Cal let his hand fall away from Reenie's arm and turned away.

"Cal—I didn't mean that." Reenie looked down, embarrassed.

"They're here."

Reenie was so engrossed in the conversation she had not noticed the truck arriving at the open area, but now its engine was chugging in neutral in the mist on the other side of the camp-fireplace. She and Cal froze. The truck engine cut, and there was the sound of a door opening. Peering through branches they saw two men, grey silhouettes in the mist, walk to the fireplace and kick at the dead ashes.

"Fog's bad today."

"Yeah, I need a break from driving in it."

A match struck noisily and one of the men lit a cigarette with a flare of yellow.

"Want to light a fire?"

"Nah, it's not worth it; we won't stay long."

"Did you hear someone shouting when we left 'Vale? Was there some extra thing we should've done? Did we forget something?"

Reenie looked at Cal. She gestured with her head toward O'Malley and mouthed, "We can still get away." Cal shrugged his shoulders. Reenie felt like shaking him.

"That's why you've been studying that register like it's a girly magazine. No, this is a normal trip. And I checked every single thing last night. There's nothing out of the ordinary."

"I thought it was that Jess girl of Bagshaw's I heard. Mighty carrying voice that girl has. But if she wanted something from O'Malley, she should have told her daddy and got it on the list. We're not a personal delivery service."

"No?" the other man's voice sounded sceptical.

The first man went on with his train of thought. "Old man Bagshaw was polishing his sports car in the yard when we left. He can take the brat to O'Malley if she wants to go." The other man grunted agreement.

Reenie looked at Cal again. He was fidgeting with a buckle on his jacket. Reenie prodded him. "We have to go," she whispered, "before Jess works out what's going on and catches up with us."

Cal suddenly leant over and kissed her lightly on the lips. "Give me the helmet for a bit so they don't recognize me," he whispered, "and hop on, quick." He moved the bike clear of the tree and got onto it. Reenie passed the helmet and climbed onto the seat, her heart pounding so hard at the very top of her chest that she could barely move. Cal started the engine with an ear-splitting roar and accelerated past the campfire where the two men were astonished shapes in the fog, skidded round the parked truck, nearly hitting it, and screeched onto the road in a spray of loose gravel. Reenie clutched Cal, hoping she would not pull him off his seat as they leaned into the bend. Her heart beat so fast with fear and excitement she could hardly breathe. The bike righted as it came onto the road. The headlight made a cone of lighted fog pointing toward O'Malley.

CHAPTER 20
FOG, CLEARING

"You know what?"

"What?"

"There's something to be said for not getting any sleep."

"Yeah?" Cassie shifted her plastic bag to the other hand. It was lighter, but still held the photo from the café, half a bottle of water and the blanket. She hitched her velvet skirt up with her other hand.

"We've done a lot of walking instead."

Cassie thumped Ivan on the arm, hard.

"Ow! That hurt. And we could have frozen to death if we stood still for long enough." It was morning. The sky was lighter than the hills; now they could see the road ribboning away from their feet, instead of having to feel for its smoothness and sudden potholes in contrast to the long grass of the verge. Frost had come in the night, and now glittered delicately on every blade of grass.

"How much further?" Cassie asked as Ivan rubbed his arm.

Ivan was about to say, "Work it out for yourself," but stopped. They'd filled hours of walking in the freezing darkness with talking. It distracted them from the cold, sore feet, and hollow stomachs. Now Ivan knew that Cassie had never been anywhere near O'Malley before, had never been on a motorbike or in a car, other than a rusty old shell made into a chook house; had not seen anything other than the town of Willowvale and its immediate surroundings.

"Why do your parents stay in Willowvale? Where are they from?

They can't have been born there," Ivan asked at a point in the night when darkness inspired frank curiosity more than daylight ever could. Thistle and Raven seemed so independent, so immune to other people's opinions. He couldn't imagine why they'd submit to the restrictions of the place, so flimsily based on…on what? Fear? Rumour? Rules for the sake of rules?

"I don't know where they're from, but they haven't always lived there. They came when Pip was a baby. It wasn't always so bad in Willowvale. There were lots of good things about it until a couple of years ago. I guess Thistle and Raven thought things would get better…and then when Pip disappeared we had to wait, wait for him to come back. We couldn't leave, even if we wanted. How would he ever find us if we were gone? They probably would have moved on, but for that…" Her voice trailed off into sadness.

They walked in silence for a while.

"You never told me why Pip ran away," Ivan said into the darkness.

"I don't like talking about it," said Cassie. "Things were pretty good until a couple of years ago, for me. I mean, there was always the worry about the crater and nobody much went to O'Malley or anywhere, except a few traders…but, you know, good enough. Thistle and Raven had a shop in town then. We used to sell musical instruments—there were dances every Friday night in the old school hall. Everyone came—well, nearly everyone. When I was quite little."

"So what changed?"

"There was an election. I was too young to understand it. After that things changed bit by bit. Then when I was about twelve they built the walls. Pip got to be friends with that horrible Jess…"

"The walls are only a few years old?"

"All the rules got bad, and worse. Thistle and Raven had to close the shop, and there were no dances and school got horribler and horribler. Then Pip ran away."

It was light now, the colourless light of an early winter morning. They were at the top of a rise.

"I know exactly where we are," said Ivan suddenly. The road curved away downward, the river that linked Willowvale and O'Malley out of sight to the west, wooded hills that were almost mountains beyond it. After crossing a small creek the road climbed to the next rise, and there Ivan recognized the place where in his world there was a roadside rest area. "We're about ten kilometres from Stirling...maybe forty or forty-five from Willowvale."

"We'll never get there."

"Yes, we will," said Ivan. "We have to, if you want to find Pip."

Cassie's response to this remark was to increase her pace. While they approached the bottom of the slope, a long finger of fog moved up from the river and across the road. It was like walking into a wet spider-web. The moist air swirled and grasped. It was as difficult as walking in the dark, and more confusing because the very air seemed to move and change around them.

The road climbed on and on, now that the ridge was hidden in fog. The mist followed them, or grew—surely it had been lying in a narrow band at first? *We must be near the top*, thought Ivan hopefully. As he walked, he tried to list landmarks between here and Willowvale in his mind. The rest stop. Another descent and climb, then the steep hill down after the road crossed the old railway line. Another wide valley to cross a few kilometres before the village of Stirling. The fog made everything uncertain. Ivan realized that Cassie was so far ahead now that he couldn't see her. Hurrying to catch up, tired, hungry, aware of his breath sounding in his throat, every lungful laced with icy mist, his weary feet crunching the gravel of the road, rhythms regular but out of tune with each other—all fighting...Ivan realized he was alone. Where was Cassie?

"Cassie! Wait! I can't see you!"

More than one voice replied, like echoes. What was there for echoes to bounce off here? Ivan turned on the spot, trying to pinpoint the direction from which the sound came.

Cassie appeared in the fog ahead. Ivan thought he was seeing ghosts. There were other figures behind her.

"Ivan! It's Thistle! Come on, hurry!" Cassie ran to Ivan, grabbed his hand and dragged him up the road. Two other figures loomed out of the mist.

"Hurry off the road," said the first, who was indeed Thistle, "we have to be out of sight when the trading truck goes past."

Ivan followed the group onto an overgrown dirt track, down a short slope past a muddy-smelling dam, and was surprised to see the walls of a house.

"Inside," said the other woman.

It was a ruin, an old pisé farmhouse. Ivan remembered it now. In his world it was fenced sternly to keep cows and curious children out. Exactly as in his world, it was roofless, with holes for windows and a doorway. Behind it was a strange buggy made of bicycle wheels and junk. Inside were three horses, saddlebags packed. The remains of a fire glowed on the dirt floor.

Cassie and Thistle were hugging so tightly that Ivan thought they'd break each other's ribs. Thistle hid her face in Cassie's wild hair.

Ivan stood uncertainly, feeling left out, as usual. Then from behind the horses, Mick appeared. Ivan couldn't stop an instant reaction; "Dad—oh, sorry." Ivan turned away and coughed to hide his embarrassment and disappointment. Not Dad. He'd forgotten. He bent down to put his plastic bag on the ground to avoid looking at Mick—and was tangled in a clumsy hug. It was Iris, the woman from the door at the dance, the one who'd let him and Cassie leave.

"We're so glad to see you," she said, "aren't we, Mick?"

"Yep," said Mick. He came from behind the horse and gave Ivan a handshake, which from what Ivan suspected was a shove from

Iris, became a slap on the back and an almost-hug.

"I've got to get back to Willowvale," said Ivan, with thoughts of Mum, Dad, Reenie, Anna, Gran and Pop, and Frankie too. "Can we go? Now?"

"Hold your horses," said Mick. "Easier said than done."

"Thistle, listen," said Cassie, "Ivan knows how to get Pip back, we found out lots of stuff in O'Malley, and—"

"Now isn't the time for talking," interrupted Iris.

"No, Bagshaw's truck will be passing any minute," said Mick.

"We'll lay low in the ruins until we hear the truck pass," Iris explained to Ivan. "Then we can go."

They sat in a ring on the floor around the remains of the small fire, which failed to give much heat. Thistle held Cassie's hand as if she'd never let it go. Ivan was a little surprised—he saw tears rolling silently down her cheeks. Thistle seemed so impenetrable in Willowvale. But she was Cassie's mother, after all. Cassie reached across with her free hand and took Ivan's.

What felt like a long interval passed in silence. Every time Cassie, bursting with the need to tell of their adventures, said, "The outsiders weren't so bad," or "We found people who know Pip," someone said, "Shh, listen for an engine," or, "We need to hear about it all, but tell us later." The fog swirled in through the window spaces and empty roof, forming droplets of water on their hair and the fur of their jackets. After the hours of walking, Ivan felt cold. He watched the fire, straining his eyes for colour, but there was only the faintest hint of red in the cracks between the coals. His stomach rumbled. He shifted his position a little. Then he heard a sound in the distance.

"There it is!" whispered Cassie.

Ivan pricked his ears. Yes, there was a vehicle approaching. He looked through the window space opposite him, which opened toward the road, and saw only fog.

Cassie squeezed his hand. "Listen. That's not a truck."

Ivan listened. Cassie was correct. It sounded like a motorbike. And it wasn't coming from Willowvale.

Ivan and Cassie both jumped up. "Wilfred!" they said together.

"Don't stand there staring. He won't see us. Run!" said Ivan.

They pounded out through the doorway and up the dirt track. They heard shouts from the others in the house, but ignored them. The halo of a headlight appeared through the mist.

"Are you sure it's Wilfred?"

"Who else would it be?"

The bike came around the last bend, a spear of bright light in the fog ahead of it. *Was it Wilfred? How could he have got hold of a bike?* Ivan's certainty dimmed.

"We have to stop him, come on!" said Cassie. "It has to be him."

They leapt up a bank and onto the road shoulder, waving like lunatics, shouting. The light wavered wildly from side to side as the rider braked and skidded. The wheels slid and rider scraped sideways along the ground, coming to a surprisingly graceful halt at Ivan and Cassie's feet.

"Oh no," said a young voice.

"Wilfred! It is you!"

In a moment Ivan and Cassie lifted Wilfred and the motorbike, which was thankfully of the small trail-bike variety, off the ground and dusted them off.

"Are you okay?"

"Is the bike okay?" said Wilfred. "Lucien helped me buy it this morning."

"Yes, it's fine," answered Ivan, not knowing for sure.

"Cassie. Come back." Thistle's voice came faintly from the ruin—but her voice was overtaken by the sound of another motor approaching, this time from the Willowvale direction.

Ivan, Cassie and Wilfred saw light brighten the fog, pointing faintly to the sky as the vehicle approached the crest from the far side of the hill. Their feet tangled and slipped in the gravel, and as they fell over each other the fog thinned. Wilfred's bike toppled over on the road again. In confusion Ivan jumped up again in full view of the road, ready to retrieve the precious bike. The sound of the engine was loud now. Ivan heard Cassie's shout over it, though not the words.

Expecting to see a delivery van full of angry townspeople, Ivan was surprised instead to see a red motor bike, shining in the weak rays of sun that pushed through the fading mist. On it were two riders. For a split second, Ivan thought he was about to see another skid and slide, but this driver was more skilful than Wilfred, and stopped the red bike safely.

"It's okay, Cassie, it's not the truck," Ivan said when the pillion passenger leapt off the red bike's seat and ran toward him. Ivan took a step back, nearly tripping over Wilfred. The person was nearly his height, thin, with long tangled brown hair under a woolly Willowvale hat. She looked vaguely familiar. But that must be an illusion: after all, Mick looked more than vaguely familiar too.

"Ivan! I've found you!"

That was Reenie's voice. His sister, who was at home right now, worried and sad.

The person ran up to Ivan at full speed and thumped into him, wrapping her arms around him like a bear and squeezing the breath from him. Ivan tried to remain upright, to keep the balance that was being shaken both physically and emotionally. "Reenie? Is it you? What are you doing here?"

"I've come to get you back," said Reenie, laughing a touch hysterically. "And now I've found you!"

All around them were shouts and movement. Wilfred dragged his bike upright again and was being hurried toward the farmhouse by Iris. Cassie and the driver of the red motorbike wheeled the bike onto the dirt track. Thistle was with them. They spoke, but Ivan couldn't hear the words.

Mick stood on the road at the crest of the hill, looking toward Willowvale. He gave a shout and ran. "Truck coming."

In a few seconds the ruined farmhouse was crowded. The horses stamped and flared their nostrils as they saw and smelt the two motorbikes. Iris moved quickly to calm them.

Mick panted as he came in, saying, "Keep away from the windows". There was a breathless silence inside the walls as the unmistakeable sound of a truck engine approached.

CHAPTER 21
WALAGU, STIRLING AND WILLOWVALE

Inside the ruined farmhouse everyone held their breath. The truck engine changed note as it neared the access track. Reenie clung to Ivan's hand so tightly that her fingers cramped. In her mind she ran through plans...what she'd say to the truck drivers, how they'd convince them to let them go, or even help them...or perhaps she and the others would overpower them and take the truck...plan after plan tumbled through her head. Then something stopped her stampeding thoughts. *That's odd*, she thought. *The truck sounds farther away—it's going past. It hasn't stopped.* The sound disappeared down the road, bumping in and out of ruts, and eventually faded completely as the vehicle climbed the hill toward O'Malley and passed over the next crest.

Everyone shifted as they realized that the truck had really gone. Reenie looked at Ivan, and felt relief pour through her, nearly as strongly as it had the moment she first saw him standing on the roadside. He wore a knocked-about bikie jacket like Cal's and looked older than last time she saw him—not wrinkled kind of older, but more grown up; something undefinable had changed. Cal stood between the two who were clearly his sister and mother. They had expressions on their faces that must be similar to hers—joy, relief, reluctance to let the moment pass. *Funny the way families look like matching sets when you see them together*, she thought, and wondered if she and Ivan did too.

Everyone took a deep breath and relaxed. The horses, which Reenie had barely noticed, though they made the small space very crowded, changed their weight on their hooves, switched their tails, twitched the skin on their shoulders, and blew heavy vibrating breaths as if to sigh with relief for the whole group.

The woman who was not Cal's mother wore a large overcoat, patched men's overalls, very old riding boots and a woolly hat that must once have been a tea-cosy. The man who'd yelled from the road began checking buckles and adjusting saddles. Reenie had hardly noticed these people in her joy at finding Ivan. The boy who'd fallen off the trail bike took off his helmet and brushed straight blonde hair out of his eyes. He had a round, pleasant face.

"Better get going then," said the tea-cosy woman, tugging at a strap and clicking her tongue to the horse.

"Yeah," said the man, pulling the reins of the other two horses to lead them out through the crumbling doorway. His voice attracted Reenie's attention. She looked properly at him for the first time.

"Dad! What are you doing here?"

"Not another one," groaned the man.

Ivan dragged Reenie back by the wrist. "He's not really Dad," he hissed, "not here."

Reenie stared. "He sure looks like him." She turned to Ivan. "You're really Ivan, aren't you?"

He nodded. "But he isn't Dad, not really. Well, it's complicated…"

"I did warn you, Reenie," said Cal.

"Yes. I saw Gran and Pop…in town…last night…I forgot for a moment. I guess I understand," said Reenie, still thrown by seeing Dad. *Not Dad.*

"We've got the horse hitched to the buggy. Let's get going," said the tea-cosy lady, poking her head through the door. To the blonde boy she said, "Are you coming with us, dear?" The boy looked uncertain.

"But we haven't introduced anyone." The girl who was clearly Cal's sister leapt forward. She was very pretty, with a tangle of gingery-blonde hair and a fur jacket that looked like a catfight. "This is Wilfred—he's our friend from O'Malley." She pointed to each person as she named them. "Wilfred—this is Thistle, my mother; you know Ivan of course, I guess you're Ivan's sister, you look just like him—hi. I'm Cassie." The girl smiled in a friendly fashion at Reenie. "Mick and Iris are looking after the horses." Iris nodded a greeting to Wilfred, Ivan and Reenie. "And this is Pip, my brother Pip! Of course you and Ivan already know him." Cassie smiled again, so widely that Reenie thought her face would split in half. "It's wonderful! Now the only person we need is Raven."

"And we'd better get a move on back to Willowvale and find him," said Thistle, "before Bagshaw claps him in irons."

"Are you lot coming?" called Mick from outside. There was a general movement to leave. Wilfred waited, holding his motorbike by the handlebars. Cal disengaged his hands from Thistle's and Cassie's and moved to get his bike. Ivan shrank back slightly as he came close. Reenie glanced from one to the other. Ivan looked wary; Cal embarrassed.

"Hi, Ivan."

"Phil."

Reenie wanted to shake them and say, "You two can be friends now," but she didn't. She was about to say to Ivan, "Cal worked out where you were," when Cassie said, "Ivan worked out where you were, Pip. He was going back to find you."

"Thanks," said Cal, and held out his hand to Ivan.

"You're here now anyway," said Ivan with folded arms, "so it's nothing."

"Sorry about, you know, stuff, back in Willowvale," said Cal.

"Um," said Ivan. Reenie wanted to push his hand forward and force him to shake hands with Cal.

Cal wiped the back of his hand across his mouth and said, "It's finished now."

"Yes, I guess," said Ivan, and finally held out his hand.

Now that the mist had lifted the day resolved into a perfect winter day of sunlight and clear air. Distant hills appeared as close as Reenie's hand. They checked the horses' gear and set off. Mick and Iris rode. Cassie rode in the horse-drawn buggy with Thistle. Reenie continued to ride on Cal's bike. Wilfred took Ivan. The motorbikes travelled a little ahead of the horses. It was difficult to keep to horse speed, and every couple of kilometres they stopped to wait. Cal and Ivan were careful with each other at each stop—over-polite. Reenie saw that Wilfred guessed something of their previous conflict.

The journey now filled Reenie with conflicting emotions. She wanted to talk to Ivan, ask questions, and make sure he was real. She wanted to get to know Cassie, and talk to Cal, and find out more about Wilfred, but between stops she couldn't communicate even with Cal, with the wind in their ears, and each stop was an awkward few minutes when everyone shuffled their feet and their words uncomfortably. On the other hand, sitting on the motorbike, clinging to Cal's back, made her feel both excited and comfortable—she wanted the journey to go on and on. The idea of returning home was looking less attractive the longer she stayed here. She might never see Cal again once she crossed the ridge next sunset. The thought filled her with dread. She leaned her cheek on his shoulder and closed her eyes.

It was interesting, Ivan thought, how his impressions of the road changed depending on his perspective. The O'Malley to Willowvale road from Wilfred's bike in broad daylight was a crumbling maze of potholes held together with decaying bitumen. Walking with Cassie through the night, even in nothing but faint light from the stars, the road had seemed okay apart from the endless climbs over ridges and descents to creeks that made the trip feel like a sea voyage over an ocean made of ground. But then, they'd been talking all the way. School. Music. Funny things that happened. Family stories. Ideas. Hopes (but not all of them). And the trip from Willowvale with the Gentlemen had been so terrifying and confusing that the state of the road was the last thing on his mind.

The landscape was different by daylight. He could see now that every forested area was covered with logs, all fallen in the same direction, away from the crater lake, and that new trees were all the same age and size.

Wilfred drove the bike down a sweeping, shallow slope of road. Cal's bike was ahead, stopped beside a massive poplar tree smashed near the ground and grown back with multiple shoots so that it looked like a giant's crown. Wilfred pulled up next to the red bike.

"We'd better wait for the others," said Cal.

Ivan got off the bike, stretched, and looked at Reenie. She was watching Cal, who fiddled self-consciously with his brake levers and accelerator.

"So Reenie, how did you get here? When did you come? How are Mum and Dad?" Ivan's list of mundane questions fought with the hundreds of things he wanted to tell Reenie—but his sister didn't seem to hear, so intensely was her attention directed at Cal.

"Ivan, can you see them yet?" said Wilfred.

Ivan looked back up the road. "No."

They stood in what had once been a village. It must have been all that was left of Stirling, the village between Walagu and

Willowvale. Across the road were broken timbers lying over the remains of foundations that must have once been the village's public hall. A flat area half invaded by deciduous trees beyond was the old cricket field.

"Reenie—" Ivan tried again.

"Yes?" At last Reenie's attention focused on Ivan. She started answering his questions as if he'd spoken a second before. "You know, they were frantic. What can you expect? Frankie came home— that cheered us all up a bit. But it would have been better if it was you."

"We'll be back soon."

"Yeah, I guess." Reenie hugged him.

"Thanks for coming to get me."

"Cal was going to come by himself. But I didn't want—"

"Here they come!" called Wilfred. Ivan, Wilfred and Reenie stood in the road and waved.

Suddenly there was the growl of an engine—Ivan thought it was Cal starting his bike—and the loud blast of a horn from behind.

They looked round and saw a shiny sports car speeding toward them, its horn blaring. Cal was waving frantically from beside the broken poplar, shouting unheard below the noise. They jumped off the road as the car passed in a spray of gravel.

"Who was that?"

Cal came running up.

The car sped away, tyres thumping into potholes in a way that could not be good for the suspension. They ran to see what would happen when it reached Mick, Iris, Thistle, Cassie and the horses. Up the road, the riders saw the car coming and had time to direct their horses toward the side of the road.

"They've got nowhere to go and he's got it in for them," said Cal as the car accelerated, spinning its wheels in loose dirt, but it passed the horses with nothing more dramatic than a cloud of dust and a trail of exhaust fumes. Thistle's horse reared in the shafts of the buggy. Cassie clung to the seat and Thistle to the reins. The horse flicked its heels and bolted down the hill, head forward, buggy bouncing perilously behind. Amazingly, Thistle's efforts brought the horse under something like control. Mick and Iris clung to their reins while their horses circled nervously, then hurried to the poplar.

"That was close."

"What the far horizon was that?"

"Bagshaw's car. Three people in it."

It took some time to calm the horses properly and untangle the buggy reins. The humans were as nervous as the horses, and moved off in an atmosphere as tense as it had been inside the foggy ruin.

Ivan took a turn riding with Thistle. Cassie rode with Wilfred.

"You wait whenever we get out of sight, remember," said Mick. "Who knows what they're up to? We'd better hurry."

Behind the trotting horse, the buggy's wheels dropped heavily into every pothole. Soon Ivan felt as if he'd never stop bumping and swaying. The buggy looked as if it would fall apart any second, made from old bicycle wheels, a frame held together with bolts of all lengths and sizes, and an old car seat and no springs of any kind to even out the ride.

The rest of the journey merged for Ivan into a stretch of jolting tedium. Thistle didn't speak. Neither Reenie nor Cassie offered to swap seats with him for the rest of the trip. Ivan felt awkward near Mick. He was jealous of Wilfred, with Cassie clinging to his shoulders on the back of the trail bike, and worried about Reenie. She was different. What was it? Why was she so fascinated with Cal? Oh. The penny dropped. Reenie was…Ivan was reluctant to think it, but the words 'in love' kept pushing into his mind. A too-adult, too-serious word to think about. Cal. He definitely didn't want to think about it, despite Cal's apology to him and his acceptance of it. He shook his head as if to get rid of the thought, like an annoying insect.

Infatuated? Was that a better word? He preferred that word, but even with lingering distrust of Cal, he couldn't see it.

The buggy ride may have been uncomfortable, but fighting the exhaustion that crept up on him from the long night's walk and everything that went before it became more and more difficult. Ivan's mind wandered backward and forward. As a change in the road surface jerked him into wakefulness he realized that this whole weird experience was full of repetitions. This road crossed many ridges and valleys, followed alternating bends to the left and right, and this was his second journey over it. In Willowvale he'd gone up and down to the ridge and back and forth to Gran and Pop's house…the feeling of going over and over things created a sensation of déjà vu that was blurring into that strange feeling of knowing things and not knowing, knowing places and people and yet not, never being sure of anything. He dozed.

At last Ivan woke and recognized the final stretch of road into Willowvale. The group met under a copse of trees near a fallen railway bridge. They were old trees. The blast that had turned Walagu into a crater and ruined Stirling had not extended as far as here.

A heated discussion began.

"We'll cut across to the ridge and down to the shack."

"No, we can't keep creeping around like bush mice. We should go right up to the gates and tell them what to do with their rules and meetings."

"Don't forget Penny and Raven."

"What about Ivan and Reenie? They need to get home."

"Wilfred can't get caught up in this mess. He's not even from Willowvale."

Ivan sat down on the ground, leaned his head on his arms, and let the words flow over him.

Another sound intruded. An engine. The delivery truck on its return journey. Here was a repetition of yet another thing that had already happened. Ivan stood up. Nobody else heard, they were too busy arguing.

"Everyone—something's coming,"

The delivery truck approached, and pulled up.

"Guys—"

Two men got out of the truck. Other than their odd Willowvale clothes, they looked like normal middle-aged men. They looked like the fathers of people Ivan knew. They probably were the fathers of people he knew.

"Hey, everyone," hissed Ivan.

The men walked over. Ivan got ready to—well, he didn't know what he'd do next.

"What's up?" asked one of the men.

There was a surprised silence. Everyone stared at the men.

"D'you need a hand?" asked the other man.

Ivan said, "We're okay."

"You sure?"

The two men didn't seem to recognize Thistle, Iris or Mick. If they did, they said nothing.

"Yes, we're fine, thanks," said Iris.

"Not too long till curfew, don't, um, delay," said the man, then coughed in an embarrassed way and turned toward the truck.

Reenie suddenly blurted out, "How's business? Any trouble lately?"

"Have you been under a rock, mate? Weren't you at the town meeting last night? You'd know that Bagshaw went too far—"

The other man coughed. "*Mister* Bagshaw. Our employer." He elbowed his companion in the ribs. "I'm sure they know all about that. Come on, Pete, if they're okay we'll move on."

"Well, if you're sure," said Pete. Everyone nodded. The two men climbed back into the truck and it bounced off down the road.

Mick swung into his saddle. "That was weird. Well, I'm going straight in. I have to find out what's happened to Penny and see if Mum and Dad are all right. You young ones have the brains to look after yourselves, I'm sure." He winked at Ivan and Reenie.

"I must find Raven," said Thistle. "Who knows what that nutcase Rex Bagshaw will do next."

"It's not all that long to curfew, to sunset, like the man said. We need to get Ivan and Reenie home," said Cassie.

"We're not babies. Like Mick said, we can look after ourselves," said Ivan.

"Yeah," said Reenie. "But we don't need to run off yet." She looked at the sky. "It's not all that late. It's our fault if Raven is in trouble. There's time to help you find him."

"I'm not going home now," said Wilfred. "No way. Anyway, Mum'll be furious with me. I'm staying till she's had time to cool off."

"Well, I say we should storm the gates," said Iris, leaping onto her horse with surprising agility, considering her rotund form.

It was strange that the deliverymen had not roused the guards, Ivan thought. Also oddly, the gates under the arched gateway were wide open. Only a young goat stood guard in the roadway, and it ran bleating away when it saw the motorbikes. There was none of the eccentric traffic of the other afternoon.

The entered the town, wary of the guard tower—but the tower was empty, and wary of watchers—but the street was deserted.

Dismounting, they led the horses and pushed the bikes down the middle of the road. *Just like a corny cowboy movie*, Ivan thought.

A roar like the sound of a football crowd floated from the centre of town. "What's that noise?" said Cassie. They hurried, the clatter of the horses' hooves echoing off the empty walls of the surrounding buildings.

Thistle and Mick tied their horses to posts and hurried ahead.

"Leave your bikes here," said Iris. She tied her horse to a 'No Parking' sign.

Ivan walked with Reenie and Cal. Cassie and Wilfred walked nearby. There was another loud roar of voices from the centre of town. Reenie's face was pale. "Raven went back when we got out of Willowvale—what are they doing to him?" She began to run after Iris, Thistle and Mick. Ivan, Cal, Cassie and Wilfred followed.

CHAPTER 22
TREES AGAINST THE SKY

Reenie tried not to look at the crowd of townspeople who thronged on the grass, pushing up against each other in their eagerness to get closer to the bandstand. The whole population of Willowvale was there, adults, children, old people, teenagers—even a few goats. Horses were tied to trees, and children and dogs ran shouting and barking at the margins of the crowd.

There was a roar of voices from the crowd. Reenie and the others pushed forward. Reenie made herself look at the stage, dreading what she might see. Would Raven be handcuffed, or locked in stocks like something from medieval times?

Several people stood on the stage under the band shell. One of them was Raven. Thistle yelled his name and pushed toward him with renewed strength. Reenie followed in her wake, shoving past those who paid her no attention as they watched the stage.

Thistle vaulted up onto the platform. Reenie stood amongst the people at its base. Another roar came from the crowd. Reenie turned around, alarmed, ready to push her way to the quieter edge of the park and head for the hut and the ridge, if only she could find Ivan. She looked for his face among the crowd and saw, expressions of almost comical surprise on their faces: Ivan, Cal, Cassie and Wilfred. Reenie didn't understand. At last her ears tuned in to the sounds of the crowd. Not angry shouts. Cheering.

Reenie spun around again. Instead of the angry, ugly expressions she expected, everyone was smiling. Someone on the podium spoke and again the crowd cheered. Reenie felt dizzy.

"Bagshaw's gone!" Iris' voice cut into Reenie's ear during a brief silence between the cheers. "You know how we saw his car near Stirling? He's run away!"

Someone started a chant—no more rules, no more walls, no curfew. The crowd picked it up and it rolled over Reenie again and again. She saw Raven on the stage. He appeared to be in charge of the meeting. At the side of the platform she saw men dressed as guards standing relaxed and smiling.

No more walls. No more rules.

No curfew…meant no drums. The drums were an essential part of getting home. Reenie saw Ivan, separated from her by several layers of crowd. Judging by his face, the same thought had occurred to him. Cassie cheered beside him. Reenie pushed her way through the people. Ivan was already heading for the empty grass at the edge of the crowd. Cassie, her attention on the platform, did not see him go.

"This is bad," said Ivan.

Reenie nodded. The crowd cheered and clapped happily, but all she saw was the sky through the elm branches, losing its colour by the second, and shadows lengthening across the grass.

"We'll never get back now," Ivan said.

Reenie didn't answer. Not far away, lying on the grass unnoticed in a streak of winter sunlight was a large, round object. A curfew drum, dropped by its drummer in the excitement. Maybe they could get someone to beat it one last time. She looked at the stage. Raven, Thistle, Mick, Iris, Cassie and Cal were there, shaking hands with a bunch of people. Wilfred hovered on the edge of the group. They'd forgotten her and Ivan.

"Let's take the drum up to the ridge and beat it ourselves. It's worth a try," said Ivan, voicing Reenie's unsaid thought. "If we put it right at the poles and stand there drumming—" he paused. Reenie gave him a look that said, you're grasping at straws, and sighed. Ivan shrugged. "What else can we do? Unless you want to stay here forever."

Reenie looked at the stage again. None of them were scanning the crowd for her or Ivan. Not even Cal. She didn't want to stay. Not even for Cal, that strange, beautiful, exciting—no. He'd forgotten her now that he was home. It wasn't her world.

Ivan leant over, inspecting the drum. It was an old bass drum like one from a brass band. They tipped it up onto its side and without another word began to roll it toward the gate that led out of town in the direction of Raven and Thistle's shack.

It was okay getting the drum to the gate, which stood wide open and deserted, as the main gate had, and out along the road past the vegetable fields that were soccer fields at home, and across the causeway to the road that led away past the shack.

"How long do you think we've got?" asked Ivan. Reenie didn't know. The road became rougher past the shack. The shadow of the western ridge crept across the valley. They could see the gully that led up to the poles—the place they had to reach. Ivan, hurrying, gave the drum a push that sent it rolling and dancing down a slight slope of the road. They sprinted after it, caught it as it pirouetted and teetered on an edge like a spinning coin, ready to fall and split its skin.

"It won't work if it's broken, you idiot."

"We're running out of time. We have to hurry."

They continued along the narrowing road, but with more care, until they reached the bottom of the flying fox. Here all pretence of a road ended. The track narrowed to a thread of a dirt path, which crossed the bottom of the valley, and wound up the steep gully to the top of the ridge. Reenie and Ivan were in cold shadow now—but the sun still shone across onto the hills below the poles.

"We'll have to carry it from here. Take turns. I'll go first, I'm the eldest," said Reenie, lifting the drum awkwardly onto her back. It was surprisingly heavy.

After a few minutes Reenie's arms and back were sore and cramped. Ivan took the drum for a time, then Reenie again. It only took a few minutes to tire of carrying it. Soon the track steepened and became more difficult, full of shadowy rocks and treacherous gullies.

Reenie lost her footing and slipped with a gasp. Unbalanced by the extra weight and unable to put both hands down without dropping the drum, she fell between two rocks on the uphill side of the track, clutching the drum with one awkwardly angled wrist.

Reenie lay with her face in the grass, her cramped fingers still holding the drum's rim. She drew a shuddering breath to calm herself. The rocks were very close to her face. Her knees were in mud. A stone pressed painfully on her shin. Ivan's worried footsteps were close. He unfolded her fingers one by one. "Is it broken?" Reenie managed to say.

Ivan took the drum and Reenie heard him place it on the track where it could not roll away. "It looks okay." He bent to Reenie. "Are you all right?"

Ivan pulled at Reenie's jacket to help her up. As she got ungracefully to her feet there was an odd whooshing sound and a shout above their heads. She nearly fell again with surprise.

Ivan looked up. "It's Wilfred! He's on the flying fox! They've come to help us."

Reenie didn't know what he was talking about. She brushed herself off and picked up the drum. Wilfred's shouts disappeared downward. If that's what the sound was. Reenie didn't believe he was really there—it could have been the sound of a bird, and a gust of wind. If it was him—Reenie tried to remember how far it was to the bottom—it was quite a distance—there was no point hanging around waiting for Wilfred to catch up. She continued up the track. Ivan followed closely, saying, "I'll take it now," but Reenie pushed on without replying.

The cable of the flying fox shook. Perhaps that was Wilfred reaching the bottom. If he was really there at all. Reenie heard more shouts, but she didn't pay them any attention. They might have been crows cawing like people. Plodding carefully but hurriedly along, watching her feet, looking a little ahead to see where the path went, she concentrated on getting to the top of the ridge as quickly as possible.

From behind, Ivan shouted out at the same moment that Reenie realized that there really were shouts. They came from above. She twisted her neck to look ahead and saw Cal careering down the path, nearly out of control. He skidded to a stop in front of her. "Give it to me. We have to hurry."

Indeed, the shadows were close to the top of the ridge. Cal gripped the drum confidently. "You go first—hurry."

Reenie and Ivan hurried. The track did nothing to make their ascent easier—loose rocks, needles of hoar frost in all-day-shaded crevices, steep sections over slabs of shiny granite. Relieved of the drum, she moved fast.

Cal shouted encouragement. "I'll start drumming where I am if I have to—go—Wilfred will catch up and help me soon."

They heard Cassie's shouts from the top of the ridge, "Hurry," and stumbled onto the last section of the track that followed the spine of the ridge out to the poles, feet pounding.

Reenie saw Cassie standing—no, jumping up and down on the spot—at the edge of the clearing where she'd first met Cal. Cassie's wild hair and fur jacket were dramatically backlit by the low rays of the sun so that she looked as if she was on fire. Reenie and Ivan skidded into the clearing.

"Pip! The drum! Now!" yelled Cassie. To Reenie and Ivan she said, "Stand there—it might work if he drums…"

"Cassie! I want to say goodbye," said Ivan.

"Pip, drum now!" yelled Cassie again. She looked at Ivan. "Is it really goodbye?"

"I don't know. Probably. I'll miss you."

"Go—don't miss your chance. Pip—what's he doing?"

The sun sat on the western trees. Reenie hoped for a crazy second that it would get caught there and never go down. Cal and Wilfred scrambled out of the path, faces red, breath rasping.

"Cassie, you've got the drumsticks—"

"Oh, no." Cassie felt in her pockets and threw a large felted drumstick to Wilfred. "I must have dropped the other one."

Cal, who had the drum, almost threw it at Wilfred. Wilfred began beating the drum, fast. Reenie stood as if trapped on the spot beneath the pole where everyone had appeared and disappeared—the place that linked her and Ivan with their home and family. But Cal was here in this world. One part of her didn't want to leave, despite this being such a strange, disquieting place full of danger and confusion. The drum beats filled her chest like someone else's heart beating there. She was aware of Cassie hugging Ivan till his bones creaked. Cal stood, looking as bleak as he had when she first saw him, near Wilfred at the edge of the clearing. Cassie released Ivan and backed away.

Perhaps the sun did pause for a few seconds. For it seemed to Ivan that while Reenie ran from the base of the pole to Cal and held him in a tight grasp, while Cal said, "I have to stay this time," while Ivan and Cassie gently unclasped Reenie's arms from Cal and Cal's from her and took her back to the pole, Cal's face as white and grim as Ivan had ever seen it, Wilfred beating the drum as if it could end the world—the sun really did seem to wait, burning its shape into the distant leaves. Then it went down.

EPILOGUE
SUNSET

Ivan stared at the school science lab bench. He didn't see the chemistry experiment except as a maze of sunlight bouncing off the curved glass shapes of flasks and beakers. He sighed. No one but Reenie knew how very difficult it was to readjust to what he now had to make himself think of as the only 'real' world.

It was six months since they returned and Ivan and Reenie's lives had now settled back into something that resembled 'normal'. Except that now, everywhere he looked, Ivan saw the shadow of the other Willowvale. He couldn't stop himself from scanning every face in case he saw a friend from the other world who'd somehow come through—Cassie perhaps with her hair tied back and a school uniform instead of her crazy fur jacket, waiting for him to recognize her, ready to laugh at his mystification. Or perhaps one day he'd bump into Wilfred at a school debating match, or see him in a team for one of the dorkier sports like rogaining or archery. He even longed to see Cal, with his swings from skinny nonchalance to menacing intensity. The austere faces of Thistle and Raven floated into his dreams as the summer mornings shortened, and every time he saw Dad or Gran and Pop, or Mrs Penny Thompson, who was often in town, he wondered what they would say if he told them how similar and yet different they were in the other Willowvale, and how different their lives were there.

Ivan's friends had been surprisingly unconcerned at his return;

happy to see him, and curious at first, but after a few days of evasive replies drifting back into their obsession with girls, sport and video games. They were slightly wary of Ivan now, which was better than before, as if in disappearing for a week and refusing to talk about it he had gained their respect. The biker jacket (which he wore as often as possible) may have been the only reason for that, he thought cynically. The feeling of isolation that hung over him before the disappearance was as strong now, though for a different reason. Oddly, his friends didn't ask after Phil. Probably they'd expected him to quietly move on one day anyway. Sometimes Ivan even wished for the old Phil to reappear and pick a fight with him, just so he could convince himself the whole thing wasn't a dream.

Soon after returning, during the family's Sunday roast dinner, Ivan and Reenie had asked Gran Pop, Mum and Dad about a meteorite scare in the past.

"No, I don't remember anything like that," said Dad.

"I never paid much attention to the news," said Gran, "it's always been too depressing. Even worse now."

"How long ago?" asked Pop, shaking too much salt over his food.

"There was something," said Mum. "I vaguely remember a scare in the papers when I was at high school. Some scientists who worked in the telescope facilities outside O'Malley reckoned there was going to be a meteor strike. My science teacher got us to do a project on it. It never hit, of course." Ivan must have looked blank, because Mum said, "You know I grew up in O'Malley and met Mick at uni, Ivan."

It was on the tip of Ivan's tongue to ask what Mum thought might have happened if the meteorite had hit, but the subject changed to Uncle Ben and the O'Malley relations, and the moment passed.

"Ivan. Pay attention," said Ms Bodley, the chemistry teacher. Ivan dutifully gazed at the whiteboard and wrote some notes in his book…aim, method, result. If only life was that straightforward.

Of course Mum and Dad still watched Ivan and Reenie as if they thought they would disappear unexpectedly into thin air at any moment. *Ironic, that.* They dropped them at school every day on their way to work, wanted to pick them up afterwards. They insisted that Ivan and Reenie phoned whenever they were out, even if they were at the school library studying or at a music lesson or working at Macca's. Little did Mum and Dad realize how close to the truth this fear was. Ivan and Reenie *had* disappeared into thin air. Hadn't they? How could something like that happen? It was a question Ivan wrestled with in his thoughts, constantly. Was he going mad? After all, it isn't something that happens. It can't be reproduced in a science experiment. You don't just find yourself in another world almost the same and yet different from your own…not unless you are a bit unbalanced…

It was the same and yet different every afternoon. Since August the sun had moved slightly south each week until now it disappeared behind quite a different hill. At least now that it was summer the days were long and it was easy to stroll out for a walk after dinner. If of course he took his new mobile phone so that Mum and Dad could find him wherever he was.

Ivan knew it was pointless. No matter how often Hugo practised—Ivan and Reenie had knocked on doors until they found the phantom drummer and begged him to play every day at sunset— nothing would happen. It couldn't.

On cue, Hugo's drums began.

He plays a lot better now, Ivan thought idly. Not that there's any point. Even so, it was a nice place to be, looking at the view, listening to the drums and the evening sound of currawongs calling to their young. Ivan sat down on a rock. Frankie sat quietly beside him, panting in the heat. Cicadas buzzed their tiny electric-tool noises, drilling through his ears and into his brain. The sun, low to the hills, was hot and too bright to watch. Ivan turned the other way and saw the trees across the clearing painted gold by the sun. Reenie came out from the end of the track, walked across to him, painted gold herself in the afternoon light, and sat down.

As the sun descended the white bark of nearby trees changed from gold to glowing orange. Reenie stood up and walked to the base of the power poles. The sun was a sliver of red cut to lace by distant treetops.

Ivan watched Reenie. Until their adventure, she'd been just his big sister, someone to play with as a child, to fight with. Part of the family—a sister. He realized now he hadn't bothered to really know her since they stopped playing elaborate games in the dirt of the back yard, or building lego cities in the sitting room at home. Now, for some reason, the way she stood in the clearing at the base of the power poles wrenched his heart.

As the sun disappeared Ivan heard Hugo's drums rise to a crescendo. He sighed. Soon Hugo would move away from Willowvale to go to university and there'd be no more drums. Nothing was going to happen. "Come on, Reenie." Ivan stood up and stretched his shoulders. "Reenie—please. You can't wait there forever."

The last rays of the sun glanced off the curve of the earth and disappeared toward the pale stars of the eastern sky. The world changed from pink to blue. Reenie stood at the base of the power poles—no longer alone. Cal stood hand in hand with her. He looked as utterly surprised as she did. The sound of drumming ceased.

For a moment Ivan had a sudden, vivid picture in his mind. He saw Reenie and Cal in ten or twenty years, standing in the same position. Still together, shadowy children around them. He squeezed his eyes shut and the vision disappeared. He opened his mouth to ask a question—then shut it. There wasn't any point. He smiled at Reenie and Cal, who were looking at each other, not at him, then turned his face away toward the slope that led away from the sunset.

"I guess I'll see you later," he said, as much to himself as to anyone else. "I'm going to Hugo's place to say goodbye." He whistled for Frankie and walked into the gap in the trees that was the path, and away from the ridge top.

As Ivan walked down the hill, hearing every dry leaf crack beneath his feet and the last calls of the birds to each other as they settled for the night as clearly as if they perched singing on his shoulders, Cal's voice floated through the still dry summer leaves of the trees. They'll be here one day—he thought he heard, like a birdcall. But, as is the way of birdcalls, it's difficult to tell exactly where they originate, or where the sounds might be going, whether made by one bird or another. And it is certainly impossible to tell what they mean.

Ivan lifted his hand in acknowledgement and walked on. Whether he went to see Hugo, or went home, it was time to choose his own next move.

www.ingramcontent.com/pod-product-compliance
Lightning Source LLC
Chambersburg PA
CBHW060549190726
48283CB00003B/937